A BUNDLE OF STICKS

A BUNDLE OF STICKS

by *Pat Rhoads Mauser*

ILLUSTRATED BY GAIL OWENS

Atheneum 1982 *New York*

LIBRARY OF CONGRESS CATALOGING IN PUBLICATION DATA

Mauser, Pat Rhoads.
A bundle of sticks.

SUMMARY: At the mercy of the class bully,
a fifth-grader is sent to a martial arts school
where he learns techniques to defend himself
as well as a philosophy
that allows him not to fight.
[1. Bullies—Fiction. 2. Martial arts—Fiction]
I.   II. Title.
PZ7.M44583Bu   [Fic]   81–8098
ISBN 0–689–30899–X   AACR2

Published simultaneously in Canada by
McClelland & Stewart, Ltd.
Composition by
American–Stratford Graphic Services, Inc.
Brattleboro, Vermont
Printed and bound by
Fairfield Graphics, Fairfield, Pennsylvania
Designed by M. M. Ahern
First Edition

For
PETE MAUSER
Blue Belt

The author would like to thank
SIFU JOSEPH A. CLARKE,
4th Degree Black Belt,
Kajukenbo America,
for his help.

There were only four more blocks to Benjamin Tyler's stop. He looked out the window of the school bus pretending to be interested in the trees and houses moving past. His throat tightened so that he could hardly swallow.

Ben had felt safe when the bus first pulled away from Hilltop School and there were still three miles to go. Boyd couldn't beat him up in front of the bus driver, he figured. Maybe if he sat real quiet, Boyd would forget about him by the time they got to Twenty-sixth.

Ben rubbed his hands across the knees of his jeans and picked at the stitching on his baseball. If he looked in the window just right, he could see a reflection of Boyd sitting across the aisle and back two seats.

Your hair's as long as a girl's, Boyd. Why don't you wear it in pony tails? Hey, Boyd, where'd you get that grubby jacket? Salvation Army? If he had the nerve, he would say a lot of things to that creep.

3

Boyd and another kid talked in low voices so the bus driver couldn't hear. Ben's ears practically pulled away from his head. Were they talking about him?

The bus stopped, and the apartment kids got off. Two more stops to go.

Next to Ben sat Charles, a third-grader who was always following him around. Ben was in fifth grade and didn't really like sitting with him, but it would hurt Charles's feelings if he said so.

"Is he really going to do it, Benjamin?"

Shut up, Charles, Ben wanted to say. "I don't know." He focused on the reflection to see if Boyd was listening.

"He says he's going to cream you."

"That's what he says." Ben looked out the window and tried to make his heart stop flopping around in his chest by thinking happy thoughts—smacking the baseball clear across the field, Daisy licking his face, the sky all blue and not raining.

"It's true," Boyd's voice boomed from behind. "Wanna watch?"

A roar of laughter filled the bus.

The muscles in Ben's neck tightened so that he couldn't turn around even if he wanted to.

The bus stopped, and three girls got off. The next stop was Charles's, then Ben's was the one after.

4

"Hey, Boyd," someone yelled. "You oughta sell tickets."

A ruler thumped Ben on the back of the head.

"Why don't you knock 'im flat, Benjamin?" Charles asked as if it were a simple matter.

Ben's shirt stuck to his back as he squirmed around in his seat. A pasture dotted with green beehive boxes and a pony tethered to a mailbox moved past the window. "Maybe I don't want to." He'd kick my teeth out or break my jaw if I tried to fight him, Ben thought. There'd be blood all over the place and I'd throw up, that's why. Leave me alone, shrimp, he wanted to say. You're making things worse.

The bus driver bounced with the movements of the bus and mouthed the words to the music that droned from the radio. It seemed as if the kids could climb out the windows for all she cared.

Charles's stop. He stood up. "See ya," he said and went to the front of the bus to wait for the doors to open.

Tell the driver, you little pest, Ben wanted to say. Be useful for once.

Charles bounced down the steps and hopped out onto the gravel road.

The driver cranked the door shut and continued to sing. Ben looked in the mirror above her head, hoping to catch her eye. Maybe he could tell her he was about to be killed by looking at her in some

6

special way. The mirror, dumbbell. Oh, never mind. You'd never catch on anyway.

Suddenly Boyd slid into the seat where Charles had been sitting and leaned toward Ben's ear.

"I'm gonna get you, Tyler."

Ben turned around and looked into Boyd's yellow smile. His breath smelled awful, as if he'd been munching on turnips. Strawlike hair hung every which way around a long, skinny face. Scarecrow, Ben thought, and took a deep breath.

Can he hear my heart pounding? he wondered. My shirt is probably bouncing up and down. Keep cool. Don't get sick, he told himself. Think about home and sliced bananas with milk.

"Just tell me one thing," Ben heard himself squeak. "What have I ever done to you?" He held his lips tight so he wouldn't throw up. Maybe he could ride the bus back to school and call his mother or make a run for the bus driver; tell her Boyd Bradshaw was going to beat him up. This wasn't even his stop.

Ben felt every face in the bus looking at him, grinning, loving it.

"You're a jerk." Boyd sneered at Ben.

The bus stopped at Twenty-sixth, belching as the doors opened.

"Come on," Craig Olsen said. "Let's get off here."

7

"I want to see this," someone else said.

Half the kids on the bus stood up and crowded toward the door. Ben was the only one who was supposed to get off. Two girls from his class looked right at him as they bounced happily down the steps.

Ben stood up and stared at the back of the bus driver's head. Moron, he thought. Doesn't anything seem strange, all these kids getting off at the same stop? If I end up in the hospital, my dad will sue. There must be some way out. Ben tried to think of something.

Boyd followed him off the bus.

"Look," Ben said turning around. "I don't want to fight. How about if we just say you win?"

Boyd shoved him sideways into the ditch, and Ben heard the bus doors hiss shut before it pulled away.

Kids closed around them in a circle. Ten or twelve had gotten off.

Ben stood up and brushed at his knees with one hand. The other still held his baseball. "If you wreck my shirt," he warned, "you're in big trouble." He cringed, wondering why he had said such a dumb thing.

"Woo-un his widdle shirt. Wouldn't that be tewibble?" Boyd grabbed him by the front of his shirt and pulled. Four buttons popped off one by one.

8

"Knock it off, Boyd," Ben hollered. "Don't make me mad." His face burned.

A wave of laughter went through the circle, and Ben looked at each of the faces. He couldn't understand why they hated him. He had never done anything to any of them.

Ben's shirt hung open, ripped. Could they see his heart pumping? he wondered.

Boyd shoved him backward until he stumbled over a rock with his arms flying out to his sides. Ben's baseball sailed out of his hand and landed in the tall grass. With every one of his yellow teeth showing, Boyd jumped on top of him.

2

Please don't knock my teeth out, Ben wanted to cry. Just hit me and get it over with.

Ben lay on the ground with his face pressed into the dirt waiting for Boyd's blow. Please let it be over fast. His ears drummed with the sound of kids yelling.

"Get him, Boyd! Cream 'im!"

Ben tried to pull away as Boyd crammed a handful of dirt into his mouth. The side of his face scraped in the gravel and his nose felt as if it were being pushed off. Dirt mixed with the saliva in his mouth until it was mud. Ben spit and wiped at his tongue. Mud slid down his throat.

Boyd jumped up and looked at Ben proudly. Sweat trickled down the sides of his face.

Ben wanted to be home more than anything else in the world, where there was someone who liked him. Looking over the rooftops he could see the maple tree that grew in his front yard a block away.

10

Ben got up and glared at Boyd. The muscles in his shoulders twitched.

"Hit him!" someone yelled.

Who, me? Ben knew he couldn't do it. He wanted to push Boyd's face in, but something wouldn't let him.

Then Boyd's knee came up and jabbed him in the stomach. Ben doubled over, burning inside. The next thing he knew his legs were flying down the road, taking him home. His eyes stung, and his ears rang. He couldn't see or feel anything except hatred for Boyd Bradshaw.

Ben ran across the yard and onto his porch. Daisy jumped up expecting a pat on the head, but all Ben could do was stumble through the doorway.

His mother rushed into the hall. "Oh, my God!" she gasped. "What happened?"

Ben choked and sobbed at the same time. "Boyd . . . beat . . . me up."

"Again?" Mrs. Tyler reached out and hugged Ben against her green scratchy sweater.

"What in the world is the matter with that kid?" she said, her voice shaking. "Why can't you two be friends? Come on into the kitchen, sweetheart, and let me look at you. You'll feel better after you're cleaned up." She led Ben into the kitchen and pointed toward the table. "Look, I baked your favorite cookies."

11

Ben looked down at the plate of chocolate chip cookies and felt his stomach squeeze together. "I can't . . . eat anything. Boyd . . . made me swallow mud." Then he added, "Please don't tell Dad."

Ben's mother pressed him into a chair, and he sat there with his shoulders bumping up and down while he caught his breath in gasps. She dabbed at his face with a damp washcloth.

"You didn't start the fight, did you, Ben?"

"No," he managed. "You know I wouldn't do that."

"Did you hit him back?"

"No. I couldn't. Don't tell Dad though, please. He's really going to be mad."

When his breathing slowed down to normal, Ben noticed that his mother's eyes were all watery. He couldn't understand why she was like that. After all, she wasn't the one Boyd had beaten up.

A few minutes later his ears stopped ringing, and it was then that the pain shot through his nose into his eyes. The salty taste of blood mixed with mud sent him running into the bathroom. Ben spit into the toilet and watched red and black swirls flush away. Then he peeked at himself in the mirror.

Long, orange scratches covered one cheek and his nose was swollen into a flat pear. He looked into his own red eyes and thought of how Boyd Bradshaw had gone home looking perfectly normal.

12

3

"You mean to tell me you just laid there and let this kid feed you mud?" Ben's father bellowed at him from his big chair at the head of the table. "What's it going to take to get you to fight back?"

Ben looked at his mother. Why did she always tell Dad everything, even when he asked her not to?

Ben's sister, Jill, who was thirteen and in junior high, concentrated on making ditches in her mashed potatoes with her fork. She glared at Ben as if to say, "Now look what you've started."

Mrs. Tyler reached over and smoothed Ben's hair. His parents could never agree on what to do about him when something like this happened. Ben didn't know what to do either. He didn't know why he couldn't fight back. Mom wanted him to be nice. Dad wanted him to fight. But neither solution seemed to work for Ben.

A memory drifted back to him from his preschool days. He had been sitting in a sandbox across from a boy with a runny nose. Every few minutes a

13

handful of sand had rained down on Ben's head, into his hair and eyes.

"Stoppit," Ben had warned as he blinked to keep from crying, but the boy didn't seem to care.

Finally, Ben scooped up a shovelful of the gritty stuff and flung it into the boy's face. It stuck in the wetness under his nose and went into his mouth. Ben remembered exactly how he had felt—delighted that the boy had gotten what he deserved. But when the screaming started, Ben's mother had rushed outside and yanked him out of the sandbox.

"Shame on you, Benny," she had scolded. "If you can't be nice, you'll have to come in."

Ben looked at his mother across the table. "Will I have to go to school tomorrow?" he asked.

"Of course not—"

"Absolutely!" Dad said, bringing his fist down on the table. "What are you going to do? Cower in the house for the rest of your life?"

"No."

"Well, then, you'll have to get on that bus tomorrow and hold your head up."

"But, Cal," Mrs. Tyler argued, "his nose."

Ben's hand went to his puffed-up nose. It seemed as if his heart had moved to the middle of his face the way his nose throbbed.

Jill refused to look at him, his mother wanted to drive him to the doctor, Ben wanted to get dinner

14

over with so he could escape to watch television, but Dad insisted on talking about Ben's problem.

"I'll tell you one thing. If I'm around next time you come home crying, I'll lock you out of the house!"

"Oh, Cal!"

Ben pushed his chair back and ran to his room.

"Ben. . . ."

"Leave him alone, Ann. He's never going to learn anything if you insist on mollycoddling him all his life."

Ben slammed the door and did a flyaway onto his bed. Even the pillow against his face hurt his nose.

For a long time he listened to his parents argue about him. Jill never said a word. He could almost see her pushing food all over her plate, wishing she could leave the table, too.

Ben let Daisy in and went back to his bed to stare at the bumps on his ceiling. When she licked his face, he did not try to stop her. Dogs are great, he thought. They never say anything, but love you no matter what.

He had almost gone to sleep when he heard dishes clattering and Jill talking about him. "Too bad there aren't lessons in fighting," she said. "Benny needs to learn how to fight."

I don't want to fight! Ben screamed inside his

15

head. I just want to be left alone.

A little while later Mr. Tyler said, "You know, Ann, That's not a bad idea."

"What?"

"Lessons . . . in self-defense."

Ben's breath caught in a gasp. Self-defense? That meant smashing boards and throwing people around!

"Oh, Cal. You know I don't want Ben fighting. Maybe we could find out why the Bradshaw boy is acting this way."

"That's ridiculous," Ben heard his father say. "Eleven-year-old boys don't need reasons for picking on each other."

"Maybe Boyd is having problems at home or with his schoolwork."

So what! I'm having problems at home too, Ben thought.

"Baloney!" Mr. Tyler answered. "Ben is going to have to work this out for himself. I think lessons could help."

Silence. Then his mother said in her I'm-warning-you-voice, "What if you send Benny to a self-defense school and they turn him into a bully? Is that what you want?"

Mr. Tyler laughed. "You can't turn a mouse into a tomcat. What he really needs is a lesson or two in courage!"

16

Ben's throat tightened and he gulped. Tears stung his eyes. Dad just didn't seem to like him sometimes. He probably wished he had two *girls*. Why couldn't Ben be tougher or braver? He felt almost as unhappy at home sometimes as he did at school.

Ben curled Daisy's tail around his finger and let the tears roll across his face into his hair.

4

A long time later Ben woke up with his undershirt over his head. Someone was undressing him.

"Lift your arms, Benny," Dad said in a nice, quiet voice.

Ben sat up while his father helped him with his pajamas. Then they hugged, and Mr. Tyler left the room. Dad could be a weird guy sometimes, Ben thought, and went back to sleep feeling that he loved him again.

The next morning he sat on the toilet seat watching his father shave. Ben liked the way he painted his cheeks and chin with foam, then shaved it off in rows.

"So . . . what do you think?" Dad asked. "I was pretty rough on you, wasn't I?"

Ben looked at the floor. Did they have to talk about this again? He didn't even want to think about it.

"Well, your mother and I have decided to look

18

into a self-defense school for you. What do you think about that?"

You and *Mom* decided? Ben knew how his mother felt about fighting. I'll tell you what I think, he wanted to say. I think it's a lousy idea. I know all about those places, and I don't want to learn to break boards with my hands or slam people down on mats.

"No!" Ben said positively. "I can't fight. It makes me sick. Maybe Boyd has forgotten about me by now. Anyway, the school year is just about over."

Mr. Tyler stopped shaving and looked down at Ben. "You can at least look into it, son." He sighed.

Boyd sat in the back seat of the bus when Ben climbed on the next morning. As soon as the kids noticed his face, they all started laughing.

"What happened to *you*?" the bus driver asked.

Ben glared at her without answering.

"Hey, Benjamin, how does mud taste?"

"You must love mud. You sure ate plenty of it."

Ben passed Charles, who wouldn't look up, and slid into a seat by himself.

"Wimp," some girl called him.

Ben tuned out their voices and studied the seams in his pants trying to think of a good plan.

He'd heard of boys joking their way out of fights

or of guys who simply agreed with everything and kept on smiling. Eventually the bully got tired of teasing someone who wouldn't tease. It worked great for a kid he'd seen on a television program.

By the time the bus pulled in at the school, Ben had decided on his plan. Boyd wasn't going to bother him any more because Ben wasn't going to let him. Maybe Mrs. Linden would even notice his face and ask what had happened, he thought. Boyd could get expelled.

"Hey, Benjamin," a sixth-grader yelled. "I hear you got wiped out."

"Yeah, I guess I did," Ben said as cheerfully as he could, trying out his new plan.

"How much mud did you eat?"

"Oh, about a pound."

When Ben went into the classroom, everyone turned around.

"Ooh. Look at his face," Celia said. "It's all purple!"

Ben looked toward the teacher's desk to see if she noticed. "Oh, no!"

"Hey, a substitute!" Patrick said.

A woman of about twenty looked up and smiled. She had soft brown hair and a smooth face.

What a rotten time for a substitute, Ben thought. They could never control kids like Boyd. They always started out by giving them warnings that didn't do any good, and by the time they figured it out, the day was over.

"All right, quiet," the substitute said. "Everyone sit down so I can take the attendance. Let's see. This is Tuesday, Show and Tell day. Is that right?"

"Yeah, Show and Tell," Boyd said. "And we never have reading on Tuesday." He laughed.

Fifth-graders don't have Show and Tell, Ben wanted to say. No one else spoke up either.

The substitute puzzled over the note Mrs. Linden had left. "It doesn't say anything here about reading. We'll have to see about that. I'm Miss Fletcher, and I'll be with you the rest of the week. Mrs. Linden has the flu."

A wave of cheering and stomping rocked the room. Miss Fletcher rapped the desk with her pencil, but no one could hear it. Eventually the hollering died down, and the faces turned toward the front of the room.

"I'm going to have to put some names on the board for bad behavior," Miss Fletcher said, "unless you quiet down. This is my first teaching job, so I imagine I'm more nervous than you are."

Oh brother, are you in for it, Ben thought, and so am I. Boyd will be able to do anything he wants.

"Did anyone bring anything for Show and Tell? Who would like to be first?"

Boyd raised his hand and went to the front of

the classroom with a huge smile on his face. Some-how Ben knew what was coming.

"I'd like to tell that I creamed Benjamin Tyler yesterday after school."

The class exploded into laughter, and Ben dropped his head into his hands. Then he forced himself to look up and laugh, too.

"Yeah," he made himself say, "it was a real massacre."

"Sit down!" Miss Fletcher snapped at Boyd. "That's not the kind of thing you bring up in Show and Tell!"

Send him to the office. He's a creep, Ben wanted to scream. Don't you know he's going to keep it up all day?

By lunchtime Miss Fletcher looked awful. She slumped down at her desk and checked her watch every couple of minutes.

Ben brought his tray to a table and looked down at a dish of chocolate pudding next to a plate of spaghetti.

"Mm, pudding," Boyd laughed. "Looks just like mud, doesn't it?"

Ben's hands tightened into fists with a fork held tightly in one hand and his spoon in the other. His chest pounded furiously for what he felt like doing. "Sure does," he said, "and I love pudding."

22

Miss Fletcher looked at Ben sadly, the way his mother sometimes did, and he tried to smile at her. He knew half a day of misery was left for both of them.

Boyd crossed behind Ben and slapped him on the head with his hand, as they all filed back into the room after lunch. "Trying to talk your way out of another fight, wimp, with all those dumb remarks?"

"That's enough, Boyd," Miss Fletcher said. "Sit down."

"Well, he won't even fight!"

"Maybe he doesn't want to hurt you." Mike Sanford laughed. "Maybe he *likes* boys."

The class rocked with laughter. Dennis Mathews leaned back too far and tipped his chair over. Everyone went wild, and Miss Fletcher stood up banging on her desk with a ruler.

Boyd pointed at Ben. "Benjamin's a faggot. That's why he won't fight."

Ben felt heat rise into his face. He wanted to cover his ears and scream.

Everyone in the class pointed at him and laughed, even John who had spent a weekend with the Tylers last summer and Cindy who had his name on her love list.

Suddenly the lights went out and the noise stopped like magic. Miss Fletcher stood with her

23

hand on the switch. The room turned gray with Boyd standing like a black paper cutout against the light from the window.

Miss Fletcher seemed ready to explode. She waited for a few seconds then asked in a low voice, "Do you know what a faggot is, Boyd?"

5

"Sure, I know," Boyd said sounding as cocky as usual.

"Tell the class what it means then," Miss Fletcher said calmly.

Boyd's face reddened. "Well, you know."

One of the girls snickered.

"I don't think I do. Tell us, Boyd. You shouldn't use words you can't define."

"You know. . . ." He laughed nervously. "A faggot is a guy who . . . you know . . . kisses other guys and stuff."

I'm no fag, you creep, Ben almost cried. The only person I kiss is my mom, and she's a girl.

Miss Fletcher waited for the class to quit laughing and folded her arms. "There must be a dictionary in the room," she said.

Shelley jumped up and got a heavy dictionary from the shelf by the window, then carried it with both hands to Miss Fletcher.

"Boyd, come here and look up 'faggot.' Read

the definition to the class."

Boyd stuffed his hands into his blue cords and walked to the front of the room. "This is really stupid," he said. "Everyone knows what it means."

"Look it up just the same," Miss Fletcher ordered, turning the lights back on.

Boyd slapped the dictionary down on the desk and pored over it, flipping pages as if he had no idea where to find "faggot."

It's an *F* word, knucklehead. Ben laughed to himself. What are you looking in the *M*'s for? Finally two other kids helped him, and together they ran their fingers down the columns.

" 'Faggot'," Boyd pronounced at last, " 'a bundle of sticks.' "

A new wave of laughter swept through the class, only this time Ben laughed harder than anyone.

"A faggot is a bundle of sticks," Miss Fletcher said. "Remember that, Boyd. Any other definition is slang."

Boyd scratched his head. "It is *not*," he said. "Everyone knows what a faggot is."

Ben made sure he was in the front of the line when the last bell rang so he could take the front seat on the bus.

"You've really had it this time, Tyler."

Bad breath moved in behind him. You smell,

you know that, creep? Ben wished he could say it out loud. No one would want to kiss you . . . boy or girl. Yuk.

Ben looked up at Miss Fletcher, who stood in front of the door waiting to uncage her first class.

"Rough day for both of us, huh?" she whispered.

"Yeah," Ben said, feeling his face go red. "I'm going to get him one of these days."

"Want a ride home? I'm going that way anyway."

Are you kidding? Ben thought. A ride home? Sure, I do. "No thanks," he said. "I don't think my dad would like it. He says I should stand up to Boyd. Besides, I have to look for my baseball. I lost it yesterday by the bus stop."

Miss Fletcher's eyes twinkled blue and green at the same time, and her cheeks, when she bent down to talk to Ben, smelled like bubble gum or even better.

"It's okay," she whispered. "We'll be there long before the bus. I'll drop you off to look for your ball, then you can walk the rest of the way home. I don't think anyone will know the difference, do you?"

"I guess not." Ben smiled. "Okay. Thanks."

"Wait for me in the office. I won't be long."

"Okay." She's pretty smart, Ben thought. She knows what will happen if the kids see me riding home with the teacher. They'll call me "chicken" or

27

"coward." Ben wished he had Miss Fletcher every day for school. She was really nice.

He waited in the office, then the two of them went out to the parking lot and got into a red Volkswagen. It seemed strange to see a teacher driving, like the time he'd seen Mrs. Linden buying cottage cheese at the grocery store. It seemed as if teachers should just be teachers.

"Does Boyd always pick on you?" Miss Fletcher asked.

"No. Only lately. He used to pick on Dennis until Dennis gave him a bloody nose."

Miss Fletcher looked in the mirror and turned onto the highway. "Well, Ben, maybe that's what you'll have to do."

He liked the way she called him Ben instead of Benjamin or Benny. "That's just what my dad says. But . . . I don't know. I just can't seem to do it. Dad gets mad at me when I don't defend myself."

"What about your mother?"

"I'm not sure. She hates it when I get beaten up, but she wants me to be nice to everyone."

"That's quite a dilemma, Ben. How do you feel?"

"I just want to be left alone."

Miss Fletcher didn't say any more, and Ben watched for the school bus as they rolled along the highway. Did Boyd notice he wasn't there? Ben wondered. Who would he pick on now?

"I'll bet that nose hurts," Miss Fletcher said, looking down at Ben's face. "Don't you get angry when Boyd hits you?"

"Yes." Sure I do, Ben thought. What did she think he was? Some sort of saint? "My dad is thinking about sending me to some sort of self-defense school, but I don't think it'll do any good."

They turned onto Twenty-sixth, and Miss Fletcher pulled up at the corner. "Is this where the bus stops?"

"Uh-huh."

"Your father may have a good idea. After all, you can't go around with bruises all your life."

"I know but . . . the problem is . . . fighting makes me feel like I'm going to throw up. Why can't Boyd just leave me alone?"

Miss Fletcher shrugged as if she didn't know the answer. Usually teachers lectured about understanding the other fellow. But Ben did understand. He understood that Boyd hated him.

6

Ben held onto the wet lump in his jeans pocket as he ran the rest of the way home. Thank goodness he had found his baseball. Dad would really be mad if he lost another one.

Slowing up at the house, Ben noticed his mother sitting in the car waiting for him. A nervous feeling came over him as if he had to go to the dentist and knew he had a mouthful of cavities.

Mom's eyebrows twisted as she watched Ben's nose come closer and closer. You'd think she hadn't seen it before, Ben thought.

"What's up? We going somewhere?" he asked, making himself sound happy. On the back seat he noticed a sack from the Sears store.

His mother pushed the car door open. "How was school? Any more trouble?"

Ben sighed. He wanted to tell her everything that had happened, but he couldn't. She would only tell his father. "School was fine," he said.

Mrs. Tyler backed the car out of the driveway

and took off. Daisy danced on her hind legs against the gate. Quickly Ben rolled down the window. "Hi, Daisy," he called and made some little noises only he and his dog understood.

"Where are we going?" Ben asked again.

"Well, um . . . kajukenbo," Mom said.

"Who's he? A new dentist?"

Mom laughed. "Kajukenbo is a kind of self-defense; karate, judo, kenpo and boxing all together."

Ben's forehead began to prickle as ugly pictures reeled through his mind. "Mom. . . ."

"Take it easy," she said. "You know how I feel about fighting, but your father might be right. You do need to defend yourself . . . somehow. I called all over town today. I even talked to a doctor who suggested a hypnotist."

"A hypnotist? You mean one of those guys who puts you to sleep by dangling a watch in front of your face?"

"Something like that."

Ben pictured an office with one candle burning. *When you wake up you will be Muhammad Ali,* the hypnotist would say. Ben could see himself hopping up to Boyd the next day with his fists up, believing he was a great boxer. Then he could see Benjamin Tyler in the gravel again with mud in his mouth.

"Hypnotism would never work," Ben said.

"I called karate schools," Mrs. Tyler went on,

"judo schools, the Boys' Club and the YMCA. They all have self-defense programs. Finally, I talked to a man at the Kajukenbo School of Martial Arts. I thought he sounded interesting," she said. "Please give him a chance, Benny."

Ben squirmed. "I don't know. . . ."

"I promised your father I'd look into it, so I did. There's a sweatsuit on the back seat for you."

Ben sank back and folded his arms over his turning stomach. If she'd already bought the suit, he figured, she was doing more than "just looking into" this. Besides, he'd already seen it all in magazines: Chinese men in pajamas facing each other like mad animals, and men crashing through whole stacks of boards with the sides of their hands. Ben knew he could never do that.

I can get into fights for free at the bus stop, he thought. Now you want to pay somebody. Maybe you just want to see me throw up once a week.

When Ben and his mother pulled up outside the school, he was even more sure he didn't want to take lessons. Who are they kidding? he wondered. This is nothing but a garage! The door was sealed up, but a handle at the bottom and little windows near the top gave it away.

They went through a side door and stood in an office on thick brown carpet. A man in a tan and green sweatsuit sat at a desk talking quietly to someone on the telephone. When he saw them, he swiveled his chair toward the wall and went on talking.

The office was decorated with plaques and diplomas and framed photographs. The picture Ben expected of the big Oriental man in black pajamas hung on the wall above the man's head.

A little window looked into another room, but from where he stood all Ben could see were white walls and pipes along the ceiling. He would have moved closer to peek, but the man hung up the phone and stood up. He was hardly any bigger than Mom, and he had brown eyes and freckles.

"You must be Mrs. Tyler," he said in a quiet voice, and he leaned against the desk as if nothing ever bothered him at all.

While he talked, Ben rolled and unrolled the top of his Sears sack. Finally, Mom reached into her purse and pulled out her checkbook.

Wait a minute! There's no sense paying if I'm not going to stay, Ben wanted to yell. He watched her sign her name at the bottom and tear off a check.

The man turned to Ben. "Looks like someone got the best of you."

"Yeah," he answered, trying to laugh a little.

"Do you like to fight, Ben?" he asked.

Okay, this is where I'm supposed to say, *Sure, I love it,* Ben figured, but instead he said, "I hate fighting. It makes me sick to my stomach." Maybe

33

they'll refuse to take me, he thought.

Mrs. Tyler looked sharply down at him.

"That's good," the man said calmly. "Once you learn Kajukenbo, you may never have to fight again."

Ben stared at him, trying to understand what he was saying. Why go to all the trouble of learning to fight if you weren't going to do it? That didn't make sense. "You don't have to fight?" Ben repeated.

The man never moved from his place by the desk, but stood with his arms folded across his chest and talked in a soft voice. "If you aren't afraid, you won't feel that you have to fight. And you won't be frightened if you know what to do, how to handle yourself."

I'm scared now, Ben thought, but I sure don't feel like fighting. Something was wrong! What about breaking things in half with your hands and flipping people over your shoulder? And so what if he wasn't scared; what good would that do unless Boyd knew it too?

The man opened the door into the other room. "Well, Ben, shall we get started?"

"Right now? Today?" Ben gasped. He had expected the man to say something like, *See you a week from Tuesday.* He looked at Mom, pleading. Please don't leave me here, he wanted to beg. I'm not ready!

"Not only today. I hope to see you here every

day, except weekends. The more often you come, the more quickly you'll learn."

It seemed as if some sort of robot followed the man into the other room, not Ben. One of his knees almost folded as the door bumped shut behind them.

"In class my students call me Sifu," the man said. "You will salute me whenever you come or go —like this." He placed one fist against the palm of his other hand and bowed his head slightly.

Ben stared at Sifu for several seconds before he realized he was expected to do the same. Then he bowed stiffly and rose again to look over the strange room.

7

A teenager with black hair sat on a mat in the corner, but he looked more Mexican than Chinese. About twelve other men and one woman exercised in sweatsuits or loose black pants. A few men wore colored belts tied around their waists. Where were the pajama outfits and the Chinese people? Where were the kids? Ben wondered.

His eyes stopped at a painting that covered a third of the side wall from floor to ceiling. A black and white circle stood out in the middle of the picture, with a weird-looking swirl disappearing into the center. To the right of the circle, a four-foot tiger's head snarled at Ben. To the left, the eyes of a giant scaly dragon seemed to pull at him in a strange way that wouldn't let him go.

What does it mean? Ben wondered. The dragon's eyes seemed focused in two different places at once, and they almost moved as he looked into one and then the other. Its gray body blended into the background as if it weren't really there.

Mirrors covered the opposite side wall where several men jumped around watching themselves thrust out their fists and kick with the sides of their feet. The woman was swinging a long pole around. They looked like tribesmen from the *National Geographic,* except without the feathers, Ben thought.

He snickered at his own joke and looked back toward the door. How long did he have to stay there? Somewhere outside he heard a car pull away.

Another man in faded jeans worked out in the far corner by himself. Each time he struck out, his face twisted into a grimace, and for some puzzling reason Ben felt afraid of him.

Ben waited by Sifu, hoping he would explain everything, but he didn't. The magazine articles he'd seen must be true, Ben thought. Karate schools were weird places. How could his mother leave him here? In his mind he saw Sifu and his students all smoking long pipes.

A shiver crawled up Ben's back. Except for the sweatsuits, nothing looked ordinary. He checked the room for a gumball machine or something else that was safe.

"Aren't there any other kids?" Ben asked finally. His own voice startled him.

"Not at the moment," Sifu answered. "I had a boy coming on Saturday mornings, but he quit. It's best to work alone at first anyway." He looked down at Ben's Sears sack. "As soon as you change, we'll get started." He pointed to a red curtain, and Ben went into a dressing room to change.

As slowly as he could, he pulled on the navy blue suit his mother had bought and thought about the Saturday kid. How old was he? Why did he quit? What did they make him do? Maybe he could stay in the dressing room until Mom came back. He could tell Sifu he had a stomachache, which was practically true.

The curtain swished, and a blond man came in to change. His arms were bigger than Ben's legs, with veins that looked like electric cords.

"Hi." He looked straight at Ben's nose and grinned as if he could see why Ben was there.

"Hi," Ben mumbled and watched him step into black pants that tied at the waist and a pair of black slippers. The man hopped up and down a couple of times and waved his arms around, then swished back through the curtain.

Ben poked his head out and considered what to do. Sifu stood all the way across the room. I have to go out there, Ben thought. If he hid all day, what would he tell Dad?

He stepped through the curtain and looked for himself in the mirrors on the far wall. His nose had turned a darker shade of blue that practically matched his outfit. Price tags hung on both the sweatshirt and pants. Quickly he pulled at them, but the little plastic strings would not break. At home Ben would have used a pair of scissors, but if they didn't even have a gumball machine here, they wouldn't have anything as ordinary as scissors either.

He tried to tuck them into his sleeves, but the strings did not quite reach, nor could he bite them in two. Finally, he crossed the floor to the instructor, trying to hide the tags with his hands.

Did he really have to call him Sifu? Why not Dan or Bob? "Um . . . Sifu?" he ventured. "What do you want me to do?"

Here, Ben, have a drag on my pipe, he half-expected him to say, but instead Sifu looked down at Ben's tags and laughed.

Ben's face went hot as the men in the room all stopped to stare at him.

"Let me help you," Sifu said, and he pulled on the plastic strings until they broke; then he messed up Ben's hair with his big hand. "Don't be so nervous," he said in a nice way.

After that Ben felt a little better. He stood in front of the mirror next to Sifu and learned the first part of Kajukenbo called the Horse Stance.

Sifu stood with his feet wide apart and bent his knees until he looked as if he were straddling a chair. Ben tried to copy him.

"Lower. Low-er," Sifu ordered.

Ben sank down as low as he could without falling backward.

"That's better," Sifu said. "Any questions so far?"

Don't you have a regular name? Ben wanted to ask. And what did the Horse Stance have to do with fighting? "No questions," he said, and he was left to practice on his own.

Ben stood with his knees apart, lowered himself down as far as he could and brought his fists in at his waist as Sifu had done. If Boyd creamed him in that position, it could be a lot worse than swallowing mud.

Soon the muscles across the tops of his legs began to hurt. "Can I stop now?" he asked Sifu, who was chinning himself on a bar a few feet away.

Sifu smiled from one corner of his mouth. "If that's all you can do, you will have to stop." He spoke in normal tones as if chinning himself were no trouble at all.

"Well, maybe I could do a *little* more," Ben said and remained in position until his legs began to quiver.

"To win your yellow belt, you will have to be able to stay in the Horse Stance for two minutes."

"Yellow belt?" Ben glanced around the room. As he had noticed earlier, some of the people wore yellow or purple or brown cloth belts tied around their waists. Sifu was not wearing one.

"As you acquire skills, you will win belts. The first is yellow." Sifu dropped down from the bar and showed Ben a chart with names on it. After each name a color was listed.

"How many belts are there all together?" Ben wanted to know.

"Seven," Sifu said. "Yellow, orange, purple, blue, green, brown and black, in that order."

Did Sifu have a whole drawerful of belts at home? Ben wondered. He must be the best if he was the teacher. Probably no one had ever shoved dirt into his mouth.

"What else do I have to learn?" Ben asked. A picture of himself in a yellow belt floated across his mind.

8

"You have a long way to go." Sifu showed Ben another chart in the corner of the room. "The Horse Stance is first, then the Outward Strike, Forward Punch. . . ."

Ben's eyes skipped to the middle of the list. *Monkey Form, Set, Concentration.* He didn't understand any of it, but nowhere on the list was there anything about fighting or even breaking boards. There must be more, he thought.

Sifu introduced Ben to one of the other men in the room. "Mike, this is Benjamin Tyler. He'll be working on the first fist movement. Show him the Forward Punch, will you?"

The man wore gray sweatpants and a shirt that said *Ski Bum* in rubbery letters. A green belt hung from his waist. A curly black beard covered his cheeks and chin.

"This one is easy," he said in a husky voice and showed Ben the Forward Punch in slow motion, starting from the Horse Stance with his fists turned

43

upward at his sides. "Just remember to turn your fist over as you strike." With a grunt he drove his big arm forward, ending up with his knuckles on top.

Ben stepped back. "Gee," he said. "I'll bet you could put holes in walls!"

Mike looked surprised. "What for?"

"I don't know." Why did I say such a stupid thing? Ben wondered, and he decided instantly that he liked Mike. He's just like me, Ben thought, except my arms look like noodles next to his.

Ben sank down into the Horse Stance and practiced shooting his fists outward one by one. It was easier than Ben had thought, and he tried to pretend he and Boyd were back at the bus stop. Maybe Dad was right. Maybe a couple of lessons could help him.

As Mike continued with his own exercises, Ben watched the other people in the room. One man in a white outfit looked as if he were fighting all by himself. First, he stood motionless with a peaceful expression on his face, then as quick as a frog's tongue he thrust out his fist.

If he could do that, Ben realized, Boyd would never beat him again. Next, the man pulled his knee up to his stomach and shot his foot out sideways. Each blow was like an explosion. Around his middle the man wore a purple belt. Someday I'm getting one of those, Ben decided. A smile spread across his face as he pictured the look on Boyd's face when he wore

44

the belt to school for the first time.

In the far corner, the same place Ben had noticed him before, the man in faded jeans punched violently at the mirror.

"Who's that guy over there?" Ben asked Mike, who sat on the floor with one leg stretched out behind him. "He looks sort of mean."

Mike turned toward the young man. "Oh, that's Warren Bogel. He started a couple of weeks ago."

Ben watched Warren strike out at the mirror over and over again, as if he were trying to beat up his own reflection.

"He scares me."

Mike smiled. "Don't worry about him. You'll still be here learning long after he's given up."

"Really? How do you know?"

"All he wants to do is smash faces. Notice he never practices the Horse Stance. He thinks he's too cool to do all that hard work. Warren wants to go straight to the rough stuff."

That's just how Boyd would be, Ben thought. Why did people like that make him feel afraid? What was it in Warren's scowl that set his stomach churning?

Ben watched in the mirror and pretended to strike out at Boyd.

Sifu appeared silently beside him. "Not that way," he said. "Don't curl your thumb under your fingers. One good blow will break it." He struck Ben's fist with an open hand, jarring his thumb painfully.

"Try it this way." Sifu moved Ben's fingers into the correct positions with his thumb in front of his knuckles. Then Sifu hit his fist again.

He's right, Ben thought. I don't feel a thing. "I never knew about that!" Ben exclaimed, and he wondered how many other tricks he would learn. Kajukenbo might be useful after all.

By the time his mother picked him up, Ben was feeling great, and he couldn't wait to get home to show Jill what he had learned.

"Go ahead, hit me," he said holding his fist up to Jill. "It won't hurt a bit. Honest."

Jill looked around to see if Mom was watching and then socked Ben's fist with her knuckles.

"Ow!" Ben hollered. "What'd you do that for?" He shook his fingers and rubbed his knuckles. "You're supposed to do it with the *palm* of your hand."

"Well, you never said *that*. I don't think you're ready to fight, Benny."

Mr. Tyler came in from the garage. "Well, Benny, how did it go? Learn anything?"

Ben wasn't going to try the same thing on him. "It went okay," he said. "But I didn't learn much the first day."

"Show me," his father persisted, and he crouched down in the middle of the living room grinning at Ben. Keys and coins jingled in his pockets as he wiggled in readiness.

"Watch out for the lamps." Mom cringed.

What did they expect him to do? Ben wondered. Throw Dad over his shoulder? He felt foolish, but he lowered himself into the Horse Stance.

Dad continued to smile as if he expected something more. "Yeah? Go ahead."

Ben pulled his fists in at his waist and threw a couple of punches toward his father. "That's all," he said. "It starts out pretty slow. You have to be there, Dad," Ben explained quickly. "Some of the guys are really good."

Dad stood up. "Well, we can't expect you to turn into a fighter overnight. Anything worthwhile takes time."

I'm not going to turn into a fighter, Ben wanted to tell him. Sifu promised I won't have to fight if I learn kajukenbo. Boyd will be so scared of me he won't dare to start trouble.

9

Dad moved Daisy out of the way and sat on the edge of Ben's bed before saying good night.

"There's one thing that worries me, Benny," he said.

Ben concentrated on the stripes on his sheets. When his father talked seriously, Ben didn't like to look at him.

"What?"

"Well, I know how proud you are of what you learned today, but. . . ."

"But what?"

"I don't think you should tell anyone about kajukenbo yet."

"Not tell anyone?" Ben looked up. "But why?" What good would it do if he couldn't tell? he wondered. How could Boyd be afraid of him if he didn't know?

"I understand how you feel," Mr. Tyler said, "but consider what will happen if you go to school bragging. The kids will want to try you out—and I

48

don't think you're ready, are you?"

Ben's good mood sank away as if his stomach were full of holes. "But Sifu said I don't have to fight."

"Well, I don't think he meant it quite the way you took it, Benny."

Ben scowled at his sheets. "What *did* he mean, then?"

"You think about that." Mr. Tyler patted Ben's head and switched off the lamp, leaving him alone to think.

Pictures floated out of the darkness into his mind, pictures of Boyd crouched down ready to fight and of himself standing helplessly in the Horse Stance getting laughed at.

Ben let out a long sigh. Dad was right. No matter how much he wanted to, he couldn't tell anyone, or he'd end up in a fight for sure.

On the bus the next morning, Boyd forgot about Ben and went on to teasing a third-grade girl named Waji. He pulled her cap off by the tassel, then wadded it up into a little ball and passed it to other boys on the bus.

"Give it to me," Waji whined. Ben could see that under her straight black bangs she was about to cry.

Boyd slapped her on top of the head with her

49

cap, then threw the pink wad to Frank Dillon. "I'll give it to you all right," he said laughing.

Frank tossed the hat back to Boyd.

Ben didn't like Waji especially, but he knew how she felt. Everyone was afraid to go against Boyd, so the hat kept sailing from one seat to the next.

Someone ought to teach him a lesson, Ben thought. Someone—but not me. Just wait, Boyd. I'm going to have a surprise for you one of these days. Ben's chest ached from wanting to talk about Sifu and kajukenbo.

Half the kids on the bus jumped out of their seats. Ben slumped down and forced himself to look out the window. I sure hope that hat doesn't come to me, he thought, or there will be trouble again.

Plop! Waji's hat fell right into Ben's lap.

"Hey, Tyler, toss it here." Boyd backed up as if he were ready to catch a football pass.

Who, me? Ben cringed, and pretended not to notice the hat, but it sat right under his nose with the pompon as big as a grapefruit.

Ben looked toward the bus driver, who seemed to be humming more loudly than usual this morning. Here, catch this, he wanted to say, or are you asleep? Oh, never mind. You wouldn't understand anyway. You'd probably kick me off the bus or tell Waji she shouldn't wear hats on warm days.

Something inside held onto Ben's arm and wouldn't let him throw the hat to Boyd. Instead, he flipped it over his seat to Waji.

"Thanks." She sniffed and smiled at Ben as she pulled the pink wool down over her ears.

Why *does* she wear hats on warm days? Ben wondered.

"Ha-ha. Benjamin has a girl friend," several kids chanted. Laughter rippled through the bus.

Ben remembered his plan from yesterday. "How can I have a girl friend," he said, "if I'm supposed to be a faggot."

The bus jolted, and the driver scowled at Ben in the rearview mirror. "We'll have no talk like that!"

He crossed his arms, steaming inside, and stared back at her. How come she never saw anything Boyd did? Was she afraid of him, too?

Ten minutes later as they filed into the coatroom, Boyd stuck out his foot and tripped Ben, who stumbled against the wall and knocked his head into Celia's coat. His sore nose pressed against a big button, and his forehead hit the coat hook.

"I'd watch it if I were you," Ben snapped, heart pounding.

"Oh, really? How come?" Boyd's hair looked even worse than usual, as if he'd just gotten out of bed.

How long can he keep this up? Ben wondered.

51

When will it all blow over? "Because . . . you'll be sorry." I'm going to get a yellow belt, Ben itched to say, which is only six down from a black belt. If you pick on me again, I'll flatten you until you can hide under a rock with room to spare. His whole body twitched as Boyd laughed at him. If only I could tell him, Ben thought. He would love to see the look on Boyd's face when he found out about the lessons.

Miss Fletcher appeared in the doorway. Ben could tell from her expression and the way she slumped against the wall that she was thinking, *Oh, no, not another day of this!*

"Take your seats, boys and girls. We have a lot to do today." She touched Ben's shoulder as he passed her. "How is everything, Ben?"

"Fine," he lied.

10

Miss Fletcher wrote the math assignment on the blackboard in squeaky yellow chalk. "I want you to do one through seven on page one hundred forty-two and ten through twenty on one forty-three," she said. "Is that clear?"

Cindy raised her hand. "Miss Fletcher, when is this due?"

"Before recess."

"Before recess?" Everyone looked around and groaned. "Mrs. Linden always lets us turn in our assignments the next morning."

"I'm sorry," Miss Fletcher said in a sharp voice. "We didn't get our work done yesterday, so we have to do it today. In addition, I want you to write a one-page story about spring to be turned in before lunch."

Boyd made his fingers dance across his desk top. "Ooh, my goodness, spring. I'm going to write about the little flowers and the warm sunshine."

Patrick laughed and spit all over his chin.

Miss Fletcher slammed a book down on her

53

desk, and the kids sitting up front jumped. "Boyd, you may do your work in the hall. Patrick, move your desk up here next to me. And if anyone else thinks it's funny, I can set up some seats in the principal's office."

Ben knew he hadn't done anything wrong, but he felt nervous just the same. Miss Fletcher was suddenly getting tough.

The room became very quiet except for the sound of Boyd shuffling out of the room. His face was pulled into a fake grin.

I wouldn't be so happy if I were you, Ben muttered to himself. You'll be pretty hungry when lunchtime comes, and you can't even spell spring.

Ben finished his math just before recess, even though it was a lot harder than he had expected. As the bell went off, Boyd flew into the room and sailed his paper onto the teacher's desk. Ben glanced at the first problem. What did Boyd think he was doing? Ben wondered. The answer was supposed to be a fraction—you know, he longed to say, fractions; those little double-decker numbers with the lines in the middle? Oh, never mind. Why should I care if you flunk? I wouldn't want you to miss recess, the only subject you can do.

Actually, Ben liked recess best too because the boys in the class played baseball. The only problem was that Boyd always named himself captain, and he picked the players. Not that Boyd was good at baseball, in fact, Ben was better; but Boyd ran out onto the playground yelling, *I'm captain,* in his mean way, and no one questioned him.

Ben knew he wouldn't be chosen, so during recess he played Four-Square with some third-graders. "Kevin, you're out," he said. "It's Tanya's turn." Ben took charge so no one would think he was playing with them for the fun of it. Instead he hoped it looked as if he were coaching.

Twice he noticed Waji peeking at him from the side of the school building. For heaven's sake, Waji, he complained to himself. Just because I gave your hat back doesn't mean I *like* you. Is this what I get for being nice? Waji grinned at him before she popped back behind the school.

Ben looked over at the boys from his own class, wishing he could play baseball with them. Dennis pitched an easy one to Mike, who swung and missed. I could've gotten that one, Ben thought. He rubbed the palms of his hands on his jeans dying to get hold of a bat.

This is stupid, Ben decided finally. Who says I can't play? Boyd Bradshaw's not King. If only he had the nerve, he would walk right over there as if that bully didn't bother him at all.

Ben watched as Boyd crouched at third base

ready to spring home. I hope you slide on your face, Boyd. It would improve your looks.

Cindy walked past him and smiled. "Gee, Benjamin, I sure wish *I* could play Four-Square with the little kids," she teased.

That does it, Ben decided. I'm not going to stand here and let girls make a fool of me. "You *can* play," Ben said tossing the ball to Cindy. "I was just leaving."

She caught it without thinking, and her mouth dropped open. "I didn't . . . I wasn't . . ." She kept talking while Ben escaped to the baseball diamond.

"Get out of here, Tyler," Boyd snarled.

Ben pretended not to notice and hollered to the catcher. "Hey, Lance, can I play?"

Lance looked at Ben, then at Boyd. "I don't know."

Boyd stepped off of third base and stalked toward him. The front of Ben's shirt almost bounced with his pulse as Boyd came near.

Maybe it's not too late to get back into the Four-Square game, Ben thought. Playing with third-graders can really be fun sometimes—and safe. Where's Miss Fletcher? Quickly he looked over the playground for someone to rescue him.

Waji stood near a tree with her toes pointed inward, watching him. Scram, you idiot, Ben wanted

56

to say. I don't need a cheerleader.

Boyd made himself as tall as he could and tried to stare Ben down, pulling his eyebrows low over his eyes.

You look like an owl, Bradshaw. Whoo! Whooo! Except owls keep their feathers neat. Sweat tingled on Ben's forehead. His throat closed so that he couldn't say what he was thinking, even if he had the nerve.

Boyd stared at him until finally Ben looked at the ground. It wasn't that he stared me down, Ben reasoned. He's so ugly I couldn't stand to look at him any longer.

"Come on, Bradshaw. Let's play," someone yelled.

"I could plaster you right now if I wanted to," Boyd bragged with his hands on his hips.

And you might get a surprise, Ben was dying to tell him. After I get my first belt, I'll be able to whip ten of you at once. "I wouldn't try anything if I were you," Ben warned and jumped out of the way as Boyd's boot came down inches from his foot.

Ben backed away. His stomach churned and gurgled until he thought it would boil over. Oh, please, not here, he prayed silently. I don't want to throw up in front of everyone. When is that bell going to ring?

"Come on. Let's play ball," someone called again. A moment later a white streak went by as Dennis zinged the ball to third base where Boyd was supposed to be.

A smile formed inside of Ben and tugged at the corners of his mouth. He tried not to laugh, but he couldn't help it. "I think you're out, Boyd." The minute he said it, Ben knew he shouldn't have. "Um

58

. . . that is. . . ."

"What did you say?" Boyd's eyes bulged, and his mouth twitched.

Whatever you do, don't run, Ben told himself. Don't let that creep know you're scared. Just walk away and hope nothing happens. "I just remembered my library book is overdue." Ben's neck tightened, waiting for Boyd to tackle him as he headed for the school.

"HEY!" Boyd screamed, and Ben jumped as his heart went crazy inside his chest. Boyd laughed uncontrollably while dizzy swirls of green leaves and blue sky moved in front of Ben's eyes. Why couldn't he fight back? One quick punch could do it, but his arms seemed frozen.

"Why are you jumping? I haven't even touched you yet." The toe of Boyd's boot connected with Ben's knee cap.

Ben grabbed his leg and groaned, unable to fight back even if he had wanted to. I hate you, Bradshaw, Ben screeched inside. One of these days I'm going to fix you good.

"Leave him alone, Boyd," someone called. "Do you want to play or not?"

"I'll play, but I'm *not* out!" Boyd returned to third base, and, as usual, no one said a word about it.

Charles rounded the side of the building. "Why don't you let him have it, Benjamin?"

"Why don't you," Ben mumbled as he limped toward the doors.

Waji watched with a sad look on her face. Go away stupid, Ben wanted to yell at her. I'm not your hero.

"I'm only a third-grader," Charles said. "What do you expect me to do?"

Ben recovered a little and stood straight testing his leg, then sagged against the school. Now he wanted to tell his secret more than ever. "You know what, Charles?"

"What?"

"Can you keep a secret?" The feeling built inside him like a bottle of warm pop and there was nothing Ben could do to stop himself from telling.

"Sure, I can. What?"

"Well . . . I've started taking kajukenbo. That's a kind of fighting like karate and judo put together. In a few weeks I'll be able to smash that bully." Ben smiled waiting for the reaction. It felt great to finally let it out.

Charles' eyes widened. Ben had never seen him so excited. "You are? How?"

"Come behind the school and I'll show you. I haven't learned much yet, but I will. I'm going to go every day. I practically have a yellow belt already."

Charles seemed impressed, and Ben felt important as he led his friend to the back side of the school. It was okay to tell Charles, Ben was sure of that. He would never give away a secret.

Ben stood behind a shrub and bent his knees in the Horse Stance with his fists at his sides.

Charles watched but didn't say anything.

Then Ben thrust out his left fist as hard as he could and grunted. He nearly fell over with the effort.

"Wow!" Charles said. "Why don't you get him right now?"

"Well . . . I don't want to hurt him," Ben said proudly. "A blow like this could be deadly, you know?" He had heard that once, but he didn't remember where.

"Really?" Charles looked at Ben with respect in his eyes.

"That is, if the wrong person were using it."

"What if Boyd takes lessons in kaju . . . whatever?"

"Kajukenbo," Ben filled in. Actually, he hadn't thought of that. What *would* happen? I'd better ask Sifu, he decided.

"They wouldn't give a yellow belt to anyone who's mean," he answered remembering what Mike had said about Warren Bogel.

"How do they know who's mean?"

"Oh, Charles," Ben sighed. "They just know, that's all. Now you try it."

Charles and Ben faced each other and Ben

61

showed him how to spread his legs and lower himself into the Horse Stance.

"Lower," Ben coached, "until you almost fall over."

Charles bounced a few times, then settled into position. "Like this?"

Suddenly giggling sputtered from the far side of the bush. Ben pushed the branches aside to find Cindy and another girl crouched down laughing as hard as they could. Cindy held her hand over her mouth and fell over when she saw them.

"How long have you been spying on us?" Ben demanded. His cheeks burned with embarrassment.

12

By three o'clock everyone in fifth grade knew about Ben and kajukenbo. Cindy couldn't wait to tell, and worse, she got it all wrong and said that Ben already had a yellow belt.

Boyd's knees wobbled and he fell against his desk. "Oh, I'm so scared. Tyler's going to beat me to death with a cloth belt."

"I'll bet he doesn't really have one," Mike Sanford said.

"Yes, I do!" Why did I say that? Ben wondered. He covered his forehead with his hands and glanced toward Miss Fletcher. She didn't seem to have heard him.

"Then why don't you wear it?" Boyd challenged.

"He might strangle you." Patrick laughed.

Nervousness mounted inside Ben. He could see where this was leading. How could he wear a belt he didn't have? "Maybe I don't want to get it dirty." A swallow rattled down Ben's throat.

Patrick and Boyd both rocked with laughter.

63

"You don't have any belt, Tyler," Boyd said.

Ben wanted to scream, *Oh yes I do,* but somehow he stopped his mouth from opening.

"If you really have a belt, then wear it to school tomorrow." Boyd jumped around like a monkey and sliced the air with the sides of his hands. "We'll have a match. Tyler versus Bradshaw. Wonder who'll win."

"Settle down," Miss Fletcher ordered. "Boyd, I want to see you after school. Every one of your math problems is wrong. Didn't you know we were working with fractions?"

Boyd shrugged as if he didn't care about the math. "But I'll miss the bus."

"That's all right. I'd be glad to drive you home."

Ben let out a long sigh of relief and sank down in his seat. Saved again. Now he would have all night to think up a new plan. But then what? Boyd wanted to see if he could really do it, just as Dad had predicted. I'm so stupid sometimes, Ben thought. But, on the other hand, if I hadn't told somebody about kajukenbo, I would have gone crazy.

Ben brightened and lined up for the bus. After all, he wouldn't have to ride home with Turnip Breath, and maybe the bus driver wouldn't have to hum if Boyd wasn't there.

"Hey, Tyler, your mom's here!"

Ben looked across the parking lot and saw his

64

mother pull up with Daisy in the car. He broke out of line and ran toward them waving. Daisy cocked her head to one side.

"Hi, Daisy," Ben called. The dog recognized him and scratched at the window so fast her paws became one gray blur. She jumped wildly from one seat to the other until Ben slid in next to his mother, then she braced her paws against his shoulders determined to lick his face.

"Ugh. Stoppit," Ben teased and hugged Daisy's warm fur against his nose.

Mrs. Tyler laughed. "I think she missed you."

"Do you want to come to school with me tomorrow, Daisy? We have an extra desk." Daisy wagged her tail and attacked Ben all over again.

He covered his face and turned to his mother. "How come you're picking me up?" he managed to ask.

"I have some shopping to do, so I'm going to drop you off early at kajukenbo. Okay?"

"That's okay with me," Ben said. "I need to learn a lot today."

"You do? Why? Did you have another bad day?"

"I just want to learn fast, that's all." There was no way Ben could tell her the truth. She would tell Dad, and Ben would be in real trouble. He hadn't been able to keep the secret even one day. The only thing to do was play with Daisy and try not to worry about tomorrow. Something would come to him, some plan that would save him once more.

They stopped in front of the made-over garage door, and Ben said good-bye to his mother. He felt a little nervous, but not as much as the day before. The silver dragon watched him enter the gym and cross the floor toward the changing room. On the way he passed Mike, who was kicking a long heavy bag that hung from the ceiling.

"Hi," Mike said smiling. "Oomph!" The bag took his blow and swung slowly to one side.

"Hi. Do you come every day?"

"Just about. I work nights at Boeing."

"Oh. I feel like that dragon is watching me," Ben said nodding toward the painting.

Mike stopped to look at the picture. "He can't be," he teased. "He's watching *me.*" They both laughed, and Ben went in to change.

Sifu was standing alone when Ben came out, and unexpectedly a plan popped into his head. He crossed the floor to Sifu and saluted as he had been shown the day before. Go ahead, ask him, Ben told himself. The worst he can say is no.

"Um . . . Sifu? I was wondering. . . ."

"Yes?"

"How long does it take to get a yellow belt?"

Sifu slung a towel around his neck. "That de-

67

pends on the individual; how often he shows up and how hard he works when he's here."

"Is there any way I could get one tonight?"

Sifu chuckled, and Ben felt his face flush. "Why do you need one tonight?"

"Well . . . there's this kid at school. . . ."

"Oh," Sifu said. "The one who flatted your nose?"

Ben's hand went to his face. "Yeah."

"And you think you might be able to scare him off with a yellow belt?"

"Well. . . ." Ben couldn't tell him he had lied about having one.

Sifu sat down on a mat and began stretching his legs, one behind and one in front of him. "Sit down, Ben," he said kindly and patted the mat next to him. "Kajukenbo is something you wear inside of you, not around your waist. The cloth is only a symbol."

"But I need the symbol tomorrow," Ben tried to explain.

Sifu's brown eyes looked right into Ben's. "What you know of yourself is more important than what anyone else thinks."

Ben didn't want to hear a lecture. He only wanted to solve his problem and it seemed suddenly as if there were just one way to do it. "Do you suppose I could *borrow* a belt? I only need it for one day."

"The ability is more important than the belt," Sifu went on.

Did that mean no? Ben wondered. Why couldn't Sifu just say what he meant so you could understand him? Ben leaned back against the wall and stared at his navy blue knees. Sifu sat quietly next to him waiting. What was he supposed to do now? Ben wondered. It seemed as if Sifu expected something.

Ben retied his left shoe and watched the other people work out for several minutes. Deep inside he felt as if there was a secret that everyone knew except him, something he was supposed to find out himself. But by that time, he might not even know Boyd, so what good would it all do? Tomorrow was what mattered.

After a long silence, Ben looked at Sifu. "When will I have the ability?" he asked doubtfully.

13

"Soon," Sifu said. "Eventually the moves you're learning will become automatic. You won't even have to think about them."

But when? By the end of next week? July? A year from Christmas?

Sifu stood up. "Have you practiced what you learned yesterday?"

"Not yet."

"You will improve by practicing every day and piling one day on top of another."

Ben stood up reluctantly to practice the Horse Stance and fist movements. Later he learned the Short Inward Block, the Long Inward Block and the Upward Block.

As Sifu showed him the moves, Ben thought about Boyd and the ways he might try to beat him. If he could somehow trick Boyd into punching him straight on, Ben could use the Outward Strike or the Short Inward Block. But he knew it wouldn't really

70

work. There was no telling how Boyd might attack him.

"What if someone hits me over the head or comes up behind me?" Ben asked Sifu.

"We'll cover that another time," he answered.

He doesn't understand at all, Ben thought. *Another time* he might not be around.

"What if someone steps on my foot or kicks me in the knee? What if they cram mud into my mouth?" Ben waited, hoping Sifu would say something more, but he only touched Ben's shoulder and walked away. Could there really be a separate move for everything? Learning would take years at the rate he was going.

An hour later, as Ben was ready to leave, a boy about his age came in. But it couldn't be the Saturday kid, Ben decided. This one looked too scared.

A mop of curly brown hair sat on top of his round face, making him look like a little kid, but he was taller than Sifu. His father led him in by the elbow, and the boy's eyes popped open when he saw Ben's nose, which had turned a bluish-green with yellow around the edges.

"Did you get that here?" the boy asked nervously.

"My nose? No. It happened at my bus stop."

71

"Good," the boy mumbled and looked around at the walls and through the window, just as Ben had done.

It hurts no matter where it happened, Ben wanted to tell him. "You new?"

The boy looked at Ben, then at his father, and said in a quiet voice, "I'm not staying."

Good, Ben thought. This kid is too crabby.

Before he went to bed, Ben stood in front of the mirror in the bathroom and practiced his punches and blocks. As long as he was just pretending, his stomach felt fine. But how was he going to feel tomorrow when Boyd jumped him? Half the class would be watching again. The only picture Ben could see was of himself with his hands over his head waiting for Boyd to beat him.

Ben tried to look at his own reflection as if it were Boyd, growling and punching toward the mirror. If only I had a belt, Ben thought. That would make all the difference. I wouldn't be scared if I had a belt.

A hand reached into the bathroom for the electric toothbrush, and Ben let out a yelp. "Watch what you're doing!" he hollered at Jill. "You startled me."

"All I did was get the toothbrush. I could've opened the door and walked right in, you know. What are you so touchy about anyway?"

72

Ben considered her question for a minute then said, "Promise you won't tell?"

"I promise. What?" The toothbrush rattled inside her mouth.

"Boyd's going to beat me up again tomorrow."

Jill stopped brushing suddenly, and greenish foam flew all over the bathroom. "What? I'm telling Mom!"

"No, don't! You promised."

"Benny, she has to know. You've only got one nose, you know."

"Dad said he was going to lock me out of the house if it happened again. Besides, I might have a plan."

Jill rolled her eyes toward the ceiling as if she didn't believe him. "What?"

"Well . . . you could ride the grade school bus tomorrow. Boyd wouldn't dare try anything if you were there."

Jill sputtered all over Ben. "That's the dumbest thing I ever heard! Ride with the little kids? I'd feel like a fool! Who would I talk to? What would I do all that way?"

"Eleven stops. That isn't so far. Oh, never mind. I was only kidding."

Later Ben had a better plan. He hung around the living room doorway until Mom's face looked just right, with a friendly, open look. "Do you think

73

you could give me a ride to school tomorrow . . . and home too?"

"What for?"

"Um, I hurt my knee, and I don't think I can get up the steps on the bus."

"Oh? Let me see."

Mr. Tyler looked up from his recliner chair where Ben thought he had fallen asleep. He moved nervously from one foot to the other, but pulled up his pant leg. He should have known she'd want to see it.

His knee looked round and pink and *normal*, with two little hairs growing out of the top. "It's mostly inside," Ben said. "You can't really see it."

Mrs. Tyler wiggled his knee cap a couple of times. "Looks okay to me," she said.

Ben glanced toward his father, who was beginning to look suspicious. "Well, okay. I guess I could hop up the steps," he said.

During the night he dreamed about Boyd, who had a giant head sitting on top of a tiny body. He pounded on Ben as if he were a wooden peg, driving him into a hole. Ben's fists flew back and forth, but he never hit anything. Sifu stood with his arms folded, watching them calmly. "You've forgotten the Horse Stance," he said and marked something down in a book.

Ben woke in a sweat to a gray morning. The

74

sun hadn't quite come up yet. Soon he would have to get ready for school unless the sweat meant something. Could he be sick? Sick kids couldn't go to school. He swallowed checking his throat. Maybe it was just a tiny bit scratchy, Ben thought hopefully. He pulled the blankets up around his neck until his mother appeared in the doorway.

"I don't think I can go to school today. I feel kind of sick."

"Oh dear," Mom said looking worried. She sat down on the edge of Ben's bed and felt his forehead. "Hm, feels normal. Let's have a look at your throat."

"Ahh."

"I don't see a thing. Why don't you get up and have a little breakfast. Maybe you're just hungry."

Ben heard his dad moving around downstairs. This would be a whole lot easier if he weren't home, Ben thought.

Jill came to the door in her red bathrobe. "What's the matter?"

"Benny feels sick."

14

Ben slid out of bed being careful not to act too happy. The truth was, if he went to school he would be sick for sure, he figured, so why go? He'd only have to come home again. Ben could see that Jill didn't believe him, but luckily she didn't say anything.

"Benny," Mom said after he'd finished three pancakes, "are you sure there isn't something else bothering you?"

Jill coughed.

"Are you embarrassed about your nose? It looks much better today."

"No."

"Then what? Did you forget to do your homework?"

"No."

Mr. Tyler came into the kitchen. "You'd better hurry, Benny. The bus will be along in ten minutes."

Ben mounted the stairs with one hand clutching

the rail. I can't go to school, he thought in sudden panic. I just can't!

Jill's chair squeaked on the tile floor as she stood up. "I'll tell you what's wrong with Benny. That creep, Boyd Bradshaw, is going to beat him up again!" Her words tumbled out, and Ben stood on the landing with his mouth open, staring down at his parents.

His mother turned white as if she were going to faint. "Why?" she asked rushing toward him.

"Ann!" Mr. Tyler bellowed. "Leave him alone. Ben will be able to take care of himself this time. He'll never learn if he doesn't try."

I'll be killed, Ben thought. This is the end.

As the bus stopped on the corner of Twenty-sixth, Ben checked the faces in the windows. Somehow he had gotten all the way from the house to the bus stop. His armpits itched and the palms of his hands stuck to his pocket linings, but it was the burning pain in his stomach that made it hard to walk.

About halfway down the bus, Boyd sat alone drawing pictures in the steam on the glass. Ben's injured nose throbbed at the sight of him. His mind raced. None of the plans he had thought of seemed right. I'll just have to tell him I forgot if he asks about the belt, he decided quickly.

There were only three empty spaces on the whole bus. He could sit with a dirty-looking second grade girl, Celia or Boyd. Some choice, he thought. Maybe I can get the two girls to double up, so I can sit alone. He held onto the backs of the seats as he made his way down the aisle toward Celia. By some stroke of luck Boyd did not look up.

"Why don't you sit with her," Ben suggested, pointing to the other girl.

Celia wrinkled her nose. "No way," she snapped.

"Come on. Please."

"No. She has bugs. You sit with her."

Ben turned toward the girl. A tangle of blonde hair stuck out over her coat collar. "She does not," Ben said. Maybe she does, he thought.

"Please be seated," the driver hollered into her rearview mirror. Then she stopped the bus for Nancy, who pushed past Ben to sit with Celia.

Swell. Now it's between Bugs and Bradshaw, Ben thought. So far Boyd hadn't paid any attention to him. In fact, he seemed very quiet, concentrating on a house he was drawing on the window. Don't you know chimneys go straight up? Ben wanted to say. And the sun doesn't have spikes, you idiot.

He couldn't sit with a girl, especially not a dirty one, so Ben finally sat down next to Boyd, with one leg in the aisle, being careful not to touch him.

Boyd continued to scowl toward the steamy window until the bus stopped in front of the school. Ben couldn't believe it. Was Boyd sick? Maybe by some miracle he'd forgotten about the belt.

"Move it!" Suddenly Boyd shot up and climbed over Ben's knees to be the first one off the bus.

"What's wrong with him?" someone asked.

Who cares? At least he's not bugging me, Ben thought. In fact, that was the best bus ride he had ever had. By the time Ben entered the classroom, Boyd was standing next to Miss Fletcher's desk talking to her very seriously.

What was going on? Was Boyd in trouble? Had Miss Fletcher talked to his mother when she drove him home last night?

Ben took a whole handful of pencils to the pencil sharpener, which was right next to the teacher's desk. None of them needed it, but he ground away until they were nothing but stubs while he listened.

"Be sure to give the office your new address," Miss Fletcher was saying. "They have to change the records whenever a student moves."

Move? Move? Ben's ears practically turned inside out. Boyd Bradshaw was going to move? Boyd's pale, miserable-looking face frowned back at the teacher. Maybe Ben had heard wrong, or maybe Boyd didn't want to leave and that was the reason for his rotten mood. That made sense, Ben thought.

If Boyd Bradshaw moved away, Ben could play baseball whenever he wanted and ride the bus in peace. Ben's forehead tightened with the sudden realization. He wouldn't have to pretend he was sick. No more nightmares. He could quit kajukenbo. His problems would be over!

It nearly killed Ben not to turn around and shout it to the whole class. Guess what? Turnip Breath is going to move! But he managed to gather up his pencils and sit down without even cracking a smile.

Ben wrestled all day with the effort of trying to look gloomy when he felt like doing forward flips. To think he had almost stayed home and missed this!

He wanted to ask Boyd if it were true, but he did not quite have the nerve. He might forget himself and break into joyous laughter, or Boyd might be reminded of the yellow belt and the match. No, Ben decided, he'd better stay away. It must be true, all right. What else would put Boyd in such an awful mood? He was probably moving somewhere really terrible.

15

Boyd moped around all day and left school the same way he came; without saying much to anyone. He never even went out to recess.

Ben couldn't believe his luck. Pictures stuck in his mind of cardboard boxes stacked all over the Bradshaws' front lawn and a yellow and green moving van. Maybe I'll be rid of him by tomorrow, Ben thought happily. Monday at the latest.

Boyd's moving! Oh, how lucky! Ben couldn't wait to tell his mother. He rode all the way home on the bus watching his old enemy's reflection in the window glass as Boyd slumped down in his seat and almost went to sleep.

Ben ran from his stop up the block and around the corner, where he could see his mother waiting for him down by their gate. She probably expected him to come home with a mouthful of mud and bleeding again. Ben laughed to himself. He waved and ran even faster while Daisy raced up the street toward him.

81

"Hi," Ben called. "Guess what?"

Mrs. Tyler's smile was visible all the way down the block, but Ben waited until they were in the house to tell her.

"Boyd Bradshaw's moving," he announced, reaching down to scratch Daisy's ears.

"Oh, really? When?"

"Pretty soon, I think. He was in a rotten mood all day." Ben took the milk out of the refrigerator and poured a bubbling glassful, then grabbed some cookies and headed for the TV. "Looks like I can quit going to kajukenbo."

Mrs. Tyler spun around and followed Ben into the living room. "I thought you liked it."

"Well, I did, but now I don't need it."

"Benny. . . ." Mom folded her arms and lowered her eyebrows. "I'm not sure kajukenbo is the right solution, but we've got to give it a chance. I've already paid for three months; and besides, what if someone just as mean moves into the Bradshaws' old house?"

"Nobody could be as mean as Boyd." Ben thought back again to the sandbox, how he had loved to make roads for his trucks and push sticks into the sand for telephone poles. The runny-nosed kid had stood outside the gate. "Can I play?" he had asked. Ben had looked toward the window to see if his mother was watching, then answered, "Go away. I like to play by myself."

"Your father wants you to go, Benjamin," Mrs. Tyler went on. "He was hoping you'd stick with it for a couple of years, at least until you can defend yourself."

"A couple of years?"

"Anything worthwhile takes time."

"But . . . years?" It was hard to picture anything taking that long; but Dad wanted him to go, and Ben knew he would end up doing what his father wanted. Not only that, but his mother had called him Benjamin, her angry name for him.

Ben swallowed the last of his milk, and Mrs. Tyler drove him to kajukenbo. As soon as he walked into the gym, Mike grabbed him and hoisted him up, bumping his head on the ceiling.

"Hi, kid. How are ya?"

"Hi."

"Wanna fight?" he teased, bracing himself in a karate stance.

"I almost didn't come today."

Mike faked a heart attack slapping one hand to his chest and stumbling backward. "Not come? Why?"

"Because . . . the kid who beats me up is moving."

Mike recovered and rested his big arm around Ben's shoulder. "Let me tell you something . . . what's this guy's name?"

"Boyd Bradshaw." The name stuck in Ben's throat.

"Well, there's always going to be a Boyd Bradshaw. As soon as one moves away, another one comes along."

Up close Mike's beard looked like a pot scrubber, all fuzzy and black. He could look scary to someone who didn't know him, Ben thought.

"Yeah. That's what my mom says, too. I guess I'm going to be coming, for a while anyway."

"Good." The edges of Mike's beard curled toward his ears as he grinned.

Sifu quietly appeared beside them, his head barely level with Mike's chin. "Go ahead and show Ben some kicks. I think he's ready," he said and moved away to help someone else.

Mike used the side of his foot, bringing his knee up to his stomach, then thrusting his foot out and jerking it back. Again Ben thought of walls crumbling in front of him. He knew he would never be able to kick as well as Mike did, but he tried anyway.

"Strike with the side of your foot," Mike coached. "And work on speed. Don't give your opponent time to grab your foot and throw you over."

Ben kicked the long, heavy bag that hung from

84

the ceiling with a thud that hardly set it swinging at all. As he kicked a second time, the bag swung to meet his foot before he was ready and knocked him down. Ben sat on the floor looking up at Mike.

"It takes time." Mike laughed. "But you'll learn. There's no need to use the bag until you're better at kicking."

For a while Ben practiced alone, using the Horse Stance and the punches he'd learned along with the new kicks. He liked the way he looked in the mirror. Boyd would be worried if he could see me now, Ben thought, driving his foot high into the air. Too bad he was moving and would never get the chance.

Ben threw a few punches toward the mirror and added a sideways kick. Even if he wasn't moving away, he'd never get me down again, Ben promised himself, and he grunted as he smashed Boyd's teeth out of the air in front of him.

"Looks good," Sifu said. He always seemed to sneak up behind Ben. "Such determination. Who are you fighting?"

"Oh, nobody. I was just pretending." As Ben spoke, he glanced toward the far wall. Just in front of the painting of the dragon and tiger, the curly-haired boy he'd seen the day before stood loosely in the Horse Stance. His knees were hardly bent at all and his arms dangled at his sides. Not coming back, huh? Ben thought. Looks like you need it worse than

I do, he wanted to say.

Sifu noticed the boy at the same time and went to show him the correct way to do the Horse Stance. Later he introduced Ben to Roger Wilmer and said that he was in sixth grade, a year older than Ben.

"We're the only kids," Ben said when Sifu left them standing alone together.

"Well, don't count on me. I'm only here because of my dad."

"Yeah, me too. But I'm beginning to like it. I hope you'll come every day."

Roger sank into a lazy Horse Stance and looked at himself in the mirror across the room. "This is stupid," he said. "No one really fights like this." He looked up at the clock. "I'm missing the *Bugs Bunny–Road Runner Hour.* I doubt if I'll be able to make it here tomorrow."

Ben didn't know what to think of Roger. Maybe there weren't any bullies in the sixth grade. Maybe Roger didn't need to defend himself. Ben watched him with curiosity. He didn't seem to care whether he learned anything or not. Did his father know? Ben wondered.

"Why don't you just watch the reruns on Saturday morning?" Ben asked him.

"It's not the same," was Roger's cheerless answer.

*   *   *

Ben looked for Boyd on the bus the next morning. From the front of the bus his eyes scanned all the way to the back. He's gone! He's really gone! Ben wanted to shout. He felt as if he were in eighth grade and six feet tall. Yet he knew that what Mike had said was true. Someone just as mean could show up tomorrow. But today he could be happy.

No one teased him about Waji or called him names. No one mentioned the yellow belt. They were the same kids, but they seemed different when Boyd wasn't around. Ben laughed and talked to Lance about baseball. Dennis asked him for a sheet of paper to make a glider. Not one terrible thing happened to him all the way to school.

Even Miss Fletcher seemed happier. Too bad Boyd hadn't moved away a long time ago.

Late in the afternoon the teacher called Ben up to her desk. "Mrs. Linden will be back Monday, Ben. I'm putting you in charge of seeing that she gets my report." She slipped a piece of paper into the top desk drawer.

Ben looked up at her, suddenly realizing that this was Friday and he might never see her again. "Are you ever going to teach school again?" he asked.

She smiled. "Sure I am. There are always a few students who make it worthwhile."

The way she said it made Ben know he was one

of those students, and he wanted to reach up and kiss her. It would have been easy with her cheek so close, but his face went hot just thinking about it.

Then an unsettling thought came to Ben: what if Miss Fletcher had noticed how happy he'd been all day and thought it was because of *her* leaving? He might have hurt her feelings when she was just about the nicest teacher he'd ever had.

"I've been in kind of a good mood all day," he explained quickly, "because of Boyd moving away."

He waited for Miss Fetcher's understanding smile—or something—but instead her face sagged.

"Oh, Ben," she said. "I'm so sorry. Is that what you thought?"

16

"You mean he's not really going to move?" Ben asked, sinking down on the edge of a table next to Miss Fletcher's desk. He had wasted two days being happy for nothing!

"He is going to move," she said, "but I'm afraid it won't solve your problem, Ben. He's moving into the apartment building on Twenty-fifth Street."

That meant Boyd would be only two blocks further from Ben than he had been before, but he would get off two stops before Ben, instead of the stop after. Ben's chin dropped so low it nearly touched his chest.

"Where is he then? He wasn't here today." Ben felt sure Miss Fletcher had made a mistake.

"I understand he has the flu," she said. "Frankly, I'm not surprised. He didn't seem to feel at all well yesterday."

I know, Ben thought. Pretty nice, wasn't it? Yesterday Boyd had kept his mouth shut all day, and today he wasn't here. And everyone enjoyed it.

A kid like that shouldn't be allowed to go to school. Ben wanted to tell Miss Fletcher how he felt, but she probably knew already.

"Oh," was all Ben could say, and he walked slowly back to his seat to stare at a scratch on his desk top. Then a happy thought came to him: if Boyd had the flu as bad as Mrs. Linden, he might be absent most of next week. It wasn't as good as his moving away, but it was better than nothing.

Ben had even heard of people having relapses, where they got well and then caught the flu all over again. If Boyd had two or three relapses he could be out the rest of the year, which was only a few more weeks.

When the final bell rang, Miss Fletcher said, "I'm sure I'll see you all sometime. Sooner or later I'll be called to substitute at Hilltop again."

The class said good-bye, and Ben hung around by the door, keeping an eye on the bus so it wouldn't leave without him.

"Good luck, Ben," she said. "Next time I see you, I probably won't even recognize you. Your nose will be the same color as the rest of your face."

Ben laughed. "I almost forgot about that," he said touching his nose. "You've never seen me looking normal, have you?" He started to walk away, then said, "Don't worry about me. I'm taking lessons in kajukenbo. That's a kind of self-defense."

"Oh, you are? Good for you, Ben." Her eyes sparkled under her eyelashes, and again, Ben thought about kissing her; but when he looked out at the bus, every face seemed to be pointed toward him.

"Well, see you," he said quickly. "It was real nice having you this week." What a dumb thing to say, Ben thought, and cringed inside. He should have told her she was the best teacher he'd ever had, or said something clever. Instead, he waved and rode home on the bus as usual.

Ben felt lonely and sad when his mother drove him to kajukenbo. He not only had Boyd back, but he had lost Miss Fletcher. He hoped it was true that she would come back someday. By then maybe he would have a yellow belt to show her. He went over and over the same happy thought until his mother pulled up outside the black garage door.

The first thing Ben noticed when he went into the gym was Roger working out with Sifu. The left side of Roger's jaw bulged a deep orange color making him look lopsided. Sifu was showing him the Short Inward Block, and Roger seemed to be trying hard to get it exactly right.

What happened to you? Ben wanted to ask, but he remembered how he had felt about his nose and didn't say anything. If he pretended not to notice, maybe Roger would tell him about it later.

91

"Hi, Mike."

"Hi," Mike said putting his fists up in front of Ben.

Ben threw his arm up to block Mike's fists, and at the same time drove a sideways kick close to his stomach. Mike laughed and grabbed him, then picked Ben up off the floor and flipped him over his arm.

"That's not fair," Ben gasped. "You're supposed to fall down." They both laughed as Mike set him upright on the floor.

"Have you ever been in a real fight?" Ben asked.

"I used to fight all the time," Mike said. "But I don't anymore."

"How come?"

"I guess I just grew up," Mike said.

"You mean you don't like to fight?" Ben smiled.

"I mean I don't *need* it."

What a strange thing to say, Ben thought. How could anyone need to fight? After all, it wasn't the same kind of thing as food.

"Hey, you'd better get busy if you're going to learn anything today," Mike told him, and Ben sank down into the Horse Stance.

Later Sifu asked a man named Greg to teach him his first Set. Ben discovered that a Set was a series of moves you did with someone else, as if you were really fighting, except without hurting each other.

Greg was short with round blue eyes and an old-fashioned haircut that rested above his ears like a wig. Hard thin arms grew out of his chest like the pipes in the ceiling.

"Grab the front of my shirt," Greg ordered Ben.

"Like this?" Ben grabbed a handful of damp blue shirt, and suddenly the palms of Greg's hands came up under Ben's elbows, a foot shot between his legs and the side of the man's hand chopped toward his neck. Ben stumbled backward, and Greg slid into the Horse Stance ready for another attack.

Ben jumped out of his way. "How did you do that?"

"I'll show you again in slow motion." Greg went through the Set slowly several times. The moves were easy, like the Short Inward Block and the Forward Kick Ben had already learned, except in different order.

"For a yellow belt, you need to know the first four Sets," Greg said, "but they're simple."

"I don't know if I'll be able to remember everything."

"You already know some of the moves. It's putting them together that counts. Just think about your opponent. He's the enemy and wants to kill you."

That part will be easy, Ben thought. Boyd's skinny face and scarecrow hair bobbed up in his mind. The only problem was, how could he get Boyd to grab him by the shirt front? How would he know which Set to use, and could he learn them fast enough? Would he need a black belt before he could really defend himself? No wonder he had gotten sand thrown in his eyes when he was five. He hadn't known any Sets!

"Ben," Sifu said later, "I want you to help Roger with his Forward Punch.

"Who, me? Okay?" It made Ben proud to know that he wasn't a beginner any more.

"You aren't going to hurt me, are you?" Roger asked.

"No," Ben assured him. "We just pretend."

"What good does that do?"

Ben sighed. In some ways Roger was just like Charles, asking a lot of stupid questions. "I don't know yet. Sifu says after a while you get so that it's automatic; someone swings at you, and you know exactly what to do."

"I don't know. I don't think it will work on me," Roger said, stroking the side of his swollen chin.

Ben thought for a moment, then decided to ask, "What happened?"

"Well, this kid at school said he was going to beat me up."

"That's just what happened to me," Ben said amazed.

94

"Then I hit the basketball pole running away from him." Roger smacked his fist against the palm of his other hand to demonstrate.

"Ooh," Ben groaned. "I'll bet that hurt."

"That stupid pole was in the wrong place. If it had been three inches to the other side, this never would have happened." Roger's eyes narrowed as if he were seeing it happen all over again. "Three lousy inches."

"It was the kid's fault, not the pole's," Ben said. "You know what I would have done?" He stopped himself because he knew he wouldn't have done anything either.

"What?"

"Oh, never mind. It's too gruesome." Ben smiled on one side of his mouth. "Well, do you want to learn the Forward Punch?"

"May as well."

Ben showed him how to start from the Horse Stance with his fists at his waist, then turn his knuckles over with his strike. When Roger tried, he looked more as if he were drying his back with a towel, rubbing it back and forth, than striking. He's never going to beat anyone like that, Ben thought. He's in worse shape than I am.

Sifu stopped beside them. "Strike with intent. We aren't learning ballet here. Even when you aren't really fighting, you must adopt a fighting attitude, or

95

you'll always be the victim." He spoke in his usual soft voice, but behind the brown eyes and freckles, he was dead serious.

After Sifu walked off, Roger's scalp wiggled. "I don't like that kind of talk," he said. "It scares me."

For the first time Ben considered the idea that he and Roger might end up being friends. They thought alike. A familiar churning brought his hand to his stomach. "It scares me too," he said. "But I don't ever want to eat mud again."

Roger looked at Ben blankly as if he had no idea what he was talking about.

17

Mrs. Linden blew her nose with a loud honk, then rested her chin on her hand and watched the students file into the room.

"Welcome back, Mrs. Linden," Cindy said, so sweetly that Ben whirled around to see who was talking.

Mrs. Linden managed to say, "Thank you, Cindy," through her stuffed-up nose, "I'm glad to be back." But if you ask me, Ben thought, she's lying.

"Miss Fletcher left you a note," Ben told her. "It's in the top drawer."

She blew her nose again and stuffed the Kleenex up the sleeve of her shiny blue blouse, then pushed her gray hair back into place. "I already found it. Thanks, Ben. How did you get along with Miss Fletcher?"

We got along great, he wanted to say. She's the best teacher I've ever had, and pretty too. "Fine," he mumbled instead.

From behind Ben a voice shouted, "Who's

sick?" Patrick pointed to an address on the chalk board written in smudged yellow letters.

Good Samaritan Hospital
407 14th Avenue S.E.
Room 213

The first thing that popped into Ben's mind was Boyd lying in a white bed with his leg tied up to the ceiling and mummy bandages coiled around his head. Maybe the moving van ran over him, he thought hopefully.

"Take your seats," Mrs. Linden said rising from her chair. "I have bad news."

Ben's scalp prickled. Quickly he checked the room to see who wasn't there. The classroom had suddenly changed. Everyone sat at attention, waiting. Who could it be? Three kids rushed in from the coatroom and slid into their seats.

"Shhh," Celia hissed. "Someone's in the hospital."

Mrs. Linden spoke solemnly as if she were in a church. "Early this morning Boyd Bradshaw underwent an emergency appendectomy."

Gasps and whispers floated through the room.

"I thought he had the flu," Dennis said.

"So did his mother," Mrs. Linden explained, "But it turned out to be much more serious."

A cold sweat stung Ben's whole body. He had wished for something awful to happen to Boyd, but he hadn't really meant it. The word "EMERGENCY" flashed across his brain in neon letters.

Celia stood up beside her desk and folded her hands. "Is he going to die?" she half-whispered. It was what Ben wanted to know too, but he couldn't bring himself to ask.

"Oh, goodness, no," Mrs. Linden said cheerfully. "The worst is over, though he won't be in school for a while. Class, who knows what an appendectomy is?"

Shelley, who hardly ever said a word, stood up proudly. "My uncle had one of those," she reported. "It was all infected, and they had to take it out." She wrinkled her nose and showed with her hands how his appendix had almost burst.

Ben looked away.

"He has it at home in a jar. I could probably bring it to school tomorrow if you want me to."

"Thank you, Shelley, but I imagine we have pictures here that will do just as well."

Craig Olsen dashed to the shelf and picked out the *A* encyclopedia. Mrs. Linden rolled down a giant chart of the human body from above the chalkboard. She pointed with a ruler to a little pink thing on the right side of the body that looked like a finger.

"This is the appendix," she said. "When the

99

appendix is removed surgically, the operation is called an appendectomy."

How long does it take to get over an appendectomy? Ben wanted to ask, but he felt too guilty to do it. Could it be his fault that this had happened to Boyd? Could wishing for something make it come true?

"I think it would be nice if we all wrote letters to Boyd," Mrs. Linden said. "He will be out of school for some time, and I know he would appreciate some mail."

What could he say to Boyd? Ben wondered. That he had wished him into the hospital? Or that he hoped he wouldn't get well soon?

Mrs. Linden passed out some special lined paper. "You'll be graded, so use your best penmanship. I'll write some of the words on the board that you might be using."

She made a list on the board of words that were hard to spell, such as "appendix," "appendectomy," "operation" and "sincerely."

How did you spell "insincerely"? Ben chewed on the end of his pencil for a long time trying to think of the right words: not too nice, but not too mean either. He didn't want Boyd to think he suddenly liked him just because he'd had his appendix out, nor did he want to get an "F" on the assignment.

"What's wrong, Benjamin?" the teacher asked.

"I can't think of anything to say."

"The best letters express how a person feels."

He couldn't do that, Ben knew. If he wrote what he felt, he'd flunk.

Dear Boyd, Don't worry about the baseball team. We can get along fine without you . . . Dear Boyd, Here are the math problems you missed. . . .

Finally, after thinking for a long time, he wrote, *Dear Boyd, I'm sorry your stomach hurts. I know how you feel. Sincerely Ben Tyler.* Perfect, he thought. I hope he gets my meaning. Not too nice. Just what he deserves.

Ben took the letter to Mrs. Linden, and she checked it with a red pencil. "This is lovely, Benjamin. Don't forget your comma after 'Sincerely'."

He smiled and said, "How long do you think Boyd will be out of school?"

"I'm not sure. He was an awfully sick boy. Let's hope not too long."

"Yeah." Ben went casually to the calendar on the wall near the light switch and counted up the days. Mrs. Linden had colored in the last day of school with a yellow felt-tip pen and edged it with gold stars. School got out June sixth. Fifteen days.

Quietly Ben sat down at his desk. Two feelings fought with each other inside his mind. Part of him felt guilty about Boyd's operation, but the other part wanted to jump into the air and yell, "Whoopee!"

101

18

Ben had never thought it could happen, but by the end of the week he had put Boyd Bradshaw out of his mind. He rode the bus, played baseball and went to kajukenbo every night after school, all with an easy mind.

Before long he was able to do the first four Sets, a Monkey Form and a Concentration, which were like Sets except that they were done without another person. He also worked out with sit-ups, a jump rope and stretching exercises. His body began to feel like a rubber band.

One day Sifu told Roger to time Ben in the Horse Stance. What was up? Ben wondered. No one had ever timed him before.

He stood in front of the dragon painting and turned his back to Roger who held Sifu's stop watch. Then he sank down into position with his fists at his sides. His legs did not feel as weird as the first time he had tried to do the Horse Stance, but the tightness in his thighs made him wonder how long he could last.

102

"Okay," Ben said with a nervous puff, "I'm ready."

Don't think about your legs, he told himself, and forced his mind onto other things: the black and white swirl between the dragon and tiger, what it might mean, the claws that looked so real. Ben studied the brush strokes, wondering how the artist had made the claws appear so shiny. Then he counted seventeen pipes in the ceiling and thirty-eight cracks in the wall.

"How much longer?"

"I'm not telling," Roger teased.

"Come on. I'm about to fall over."

"Not too much longer."

The muscles in Ben's thighs began to twitch. It sure would feel good to sit down, he thought, before he fell down. His legs burned from his knees to his stomach.

"Aren't my two minutes up yet?" Ben doubled and undoubled his fists wanting to rub his legs. A long silence filled the space.

"Roger . . . how much longer?"

"Um . . . I lost track. Let's see, the hand went around once and then. . . ."

"For crying out loud. I'm going to collapse." Ben gritted his teeth hoping Sifu would do something to help him.

Roger went on mumbling about the stop watch.

"And then it passed the four and. . . ."

Ben looked into the dragon's eyes and tried to force his mind to go somewhere else, somewhere that didn't hurt so much.

Finally Sifu appeared beside him, and Ben waited for him to say he could quit. "Make friends with the pain," the instructor said softly. "You will live through it."

Make friends with pain? That was the weirdest thing he had ever heard, Ben thought. When could he stop? His eyes seemed to bulge, then they crossed and his nose became a pinkish blur in front of him.

"Three minutes," Roger called out.

"Three?" Ben struggled to stand up and to reach for Roger, but he didn't have the strength to do anything to him, even if he wanted to. "It was only supposed to be *two* minutes!" Ben complained with a gasp.

Roger frowned and traced his finger around the watch. "Or was it four?"

Ben was still shaking when Sifu asked him how many sit-ups he thought he could do.

"I don't know. Not too many right now."

"Try for thirty.

Ben started to tell him he couldn't do it, then stopped himself. "Can't" was one word he didn't want to say to Sifu. "I'll try," he said, even though he was sure he couldn't.

Roger held Ben's feet down. "You can do it," he said confidently. "I'll count for you."

"No thanks," Ben said and locked his fingers behind his head as he rolled up and down. A few minutes later he realized he had managed twenty-three sit-ups.

"Come on. Just a few more," Roger coached, then he began pumping Ben's feet as if he could somehow blow him up like a bicycle tire.

"Knock it off!" Ben gasped. "I'm going to make it by myself. Don't try to help me. Twenty-eight, twenty-nine, thirty. I can't believe it!" he said. "I didn't think I could do that many."

Sifu smiled at Ben with satisfaction. "Now let's see your Sets."

What was going on? Ben wondered. Was this a test?

He moved through the four Sets he had learned with Roger, then did the Monkey Form and Concentration alone.

"Okay," Sifu said. "Do you know who the founder of the system is and who my Sifu was?"

"No."

"I'll tell you then. Sijo Adriano Emperado founded kajukenbo in Hawaii in 1947. My Sifu was Sigung Antonio Ramos. Who is the founder of the system?" Sifu repeated.

This was weird, Ben thought. He had never

taken a test before where they gave you the answers. "Sijo Adriano Emperado," he recited. "And your Sifu was Sigung Antonio Ramos."

Sifu said, "Good," and disappeared into his office. When he came out again, he held a yellow belt all folded up neatly with a paper band around it.

"Here." He broke the tie and tossed the belt to Ben. "You are now a Yellow Belt."

"That's all there is to it?" Ben unfolded the belt, and Sifu showed him how to wrap it around his waist.

"When you go up for your purple belt it gets a little more complicated," he said. "The promotion takes all day, with a candlelight ceremony in the evening. Yellow and Orange are only the basics."

Ben looked down at the belt tied in a giant stiff knot, with the ends hanging past his knees. He had waited all this time just to have a belt tossed to him as if it were nothing more than an apple?

From somewhere inside a strange feeling came over him, a feeling of disappointment. Except for this yellow thing tied around his waist, he was still the same person. He still didn't want to fight, and he didn't feel any braver than he ever had. Something was wrong. He should feel different. He shouldn't be wearing this belt.

Ben started to take it off when Mike approached

106

to shake his hand. "Congratulations," he said. "You deserve it."

Ben's face went hot. No, I don't, he thought. He had fooled everyone. And when Sifu found out he still couldn't fight, he'd take the belt away.

The happy feeling Ben had had earlier that day seemed to sift away through his toes. He couldn't bring himself to look at Roger, who was smiling and congratulating him.

"Hey, that's great," Roger said touching the yellow cloth. "Don't you feel terrific?"

"Well . . . it's not like I thought it would be."

"But you're happy, aren't you?"

"Sure, I guess."

Ben hid the belt in his bag on the way home and hardly said a word to his mother. You should have to win a battle before you could get a yellow belt, Ben decided. Then you'd know for sure that you could do it. He had a yellow belt, and he was still a lousy bundle of sticks.

19

Mr. Tyler pulled his chair up to the table and reached for a bowl of meatballs. Ben watched him plop four, five, six of them on top of his rice, then drizzle gravy over the whole mound. The steaming brown lava seeped down the edges and ran into his peas.

The only part of the meal that looked appetizing to Ben was the salad: fruit cocktail wiggling in squares of Jell-o. What's wrong with me? Ben wondered. I finally got my yellow belt. I'm supposed to be happy. He took one meatball and stared at it while the feeling of doom spread through him.

"So . . . how was kajukenbo?" Dad asked.

Every night at dinner he asked Ben the same thing.

"Fine."

"Learn anything new? Pass the rolls," Dad said to Jill.

"No."

"What'd you do then?"

"Oh . . . stuff."

109

Mr. Tyler looked at his wife, and they both looked at Ben. Jill reached for the salt and said, "Hey, Benny, what's that yellow thing under your bed?"

Ben's head snapped around so fast he heard a cracking sound in his neck. He glared at Jill. "What yellow thing?"

"That thing that looks like a yellow bathrobe strap."

"It's no bathrobe strap," Ben said. "It's a . . ."

"Benny." Mr. Tyler smiled. "Did you get your yellow belt today?" His mouth stretched clear across his face. "Why didn't you tell us?"

Ben flattened his Jell-o with his spoon to stop it from wiggling. "It doesn't really mean anything," he said.

"Not mean anything!" His mother sounded shocked. "Of course it does."

"Why do you say that, son?" Dad asked.

"Because . . . I still can't fight."

His parents looked at each other again. "I've seen the Sets you've learned. I'll bet you could fight if you wanted to," Dad said.

Ben tried to read the disappointment in his father's face. Was it because of him? or the money that had been wasted?

"I don't want to fight. I told you that before." Ben's eyes stung, and he considered running to his bedroom with Daisy, but he forced himself to stay and face his father. "I can't be like you," he said. "I'm just not a fighter."

Mrs. Tyler broke in. "It sounds to me as if you need to have a talk with your Sifu. I'll bet he could help you sort out your feelings."

I know what my feelings are, Ben thought, and they're sorted just fine. It was just that no one understood.

The next day Ben went into kajukenbo rubbing his sweaty palms on his pants legs. He was not in the mood for Mike, who picked him up and bumped his head on the ceiling.

"Hi, kid," he said, laughing as he put Ben down again. "Where's your new belt? You're supposed to wear it."

"I guess I forgot it. Where's Sifu? I gotta talk to him about something."

Mike focused on a spot behind Ben's head where Sifu had appeared silently.

"What's on your mind, Ben?" the instructor asked.

Did Sifu make himself invisible? Ben wondered. He was always sneaking up, appearing out of nowhere. "Um, I've got kind of a problem. My mom thinks I should talk to you about it."

Sifu led him to the mats next to the dragon

111

picture, where they sat down cross-legged. He said nothing but waited for Ben to talk.

"It's about the yellow belt. I'm supposed to be happy, but I'm not." Ben hesitated before he continued the next part. What would Sifu think of him? "I never learned anything," Ben said. "I still can't fight."

Sifu leaned back against the wall. "You learned the first four Sets, the first Concentration and Monkey Form. You learned how to endure pain in the Horse Stance. You could fight if you had to, Ben. You just don't know it yet."

"What do you mean?"

"When you know you can fight, you won't have to," he said. "But some people have to prove it to themselves before they can believe it. Maybe you're one of those people."

Ben stared at the mat for a long time, noticing the gray buttons that held it together. "You mean I'm going to have to get into a fight, don't you?"

"Well, I'm not suggesting you go out and pick a fight. There are too many bullies in the world trying to prove how tough they are. But sooner or later something will make you angry enough and you'll defend yourself without even thinking about it. Maybe it won't happen until you're twenty years old."

Ben's stomach squeezed together, and the skin

on his arms prickled. Sifu's words sounded like a curse. One way or another he was going to have to fight. "You just don't understand how I feel," Ben mumbled finally.

"Don't I?" Sifu sat up. "Why do you think I'm here?"

Ben eyed the bulges in his arms. Sifu could probably do a thousand push-ups, Ben thought; and nothing ever bothered him. It wasn't the same.

"When I was your age, I was the smallest boy in my class. I was even smaller than the girls, and I was sick all the time. You only have one kid picking on you. I had a whole class against me."

"Really?" Ben had never thought about Sifu being a little kid. "That's awful. What did you do?"

"I tried to make friends with them, I tried to ignore them—and I worried a lot; but when you come up against someone who's itching to fight, there isn't much you can do but show him it isn't worth the risk. Next time he'll think twice."

Sifu smiled as if he had some wonderful secret. "You don't have to beat a bully, you only have to hurt him. Remember that and you'll be all right."

"I don't know," Ben said. "It just seems different for me. For one thing, fighting makes me feel as if I'm going to throw up. Even thinking about it makes me sick."

"Well, Ben, you won't *die* from throwing up."

113

Just then the door opened, and Roger entered the gym. He saluted Sifu and shot a look at Ben that asked what's going on? Then he went through the curtain into the changing room and spied on them through the crack. Ben noticed his eye blinking between the folds of the curtain and tried to wave him away.

"There are two parts to self-defense, Ben," Sifu went on. "One is the physical part: being able to do the moves, being physically fit. The other part is mental, controlling what goes on in your mind. Neither part can exist without the other. No matter how well you know your Sets, if you're still afraid it's all wasted."

He stood up and pointed to the black and white swirl between the dragon and the tiger. "The *Yin Yang* is my symbol of the Emerging Center. You are working toward bringing these two sides together." As he said it he put his fist against the palm of his left hand.

Ben looked at the symbol for a while trying to see himself as a grown-up, talking softly with nothing bothering him at all. Will I ever be able to ride the bus without feeling scared? Ben wondered, or look at Boyd without my heart jumping into my throat?

"How long does it take?" Ben asked.

Sifu smiled. "I don't know yet. I'm still working on it myself."

20

Everything Sifu said sounded true. It was only later, when Ben was alone in his bedroom, that he doubted him. Maybe he means *most* people, Ben thought. Someday Sifu would shake his head and say, I just don't understand it. Ben Tyler is the only student I've ever taught who has a black belt and still can't fight. Mr. Tyler, I'm refunding your four million dollars. You may as well spend it on a house with a swimming pool, because Ben is hopeless.

A week later Ben walked into his classroom tossing a brand new baseball into the air and catching it, trying to break it in before recess. He had hardly thought about Boyd Bradshaw for a long time, and none of the kids had mentioned him since the day the class wrote the letters. No one seemed to have missed him.

The first thing he saw was the back of Boyd's head; scarecrow hair sticking out over a red collar. Boyd turned around as if he could feel someone's eyes boring into him and stared at Ben. For a second they just looked at each other.

Remembering the gritty feel of dirt between his teeth nearly gagged Ben all over again. What are you doing here, Bradshaw? Couldn't you have stayed home a few more days? School is almost over. The words swam through Ben's mind, but he didn't speak.

"Hey, Bradshaw. You're back!" Dennis shouted as if it were the biggest day in his life. "Let's see your scar."

Celia leaned on Boyd's desk and asked silly questions. "Did it hurt? Were you awake when they cut the hole? Do you have stitches?"

"Don't touch me," Boyd warned, looking very pleased with himself. "I could pop open any time."

Celia jumped back.

"Ooh, gross!" Lance groaned, holding his stomach.

All day Boyd walked around acting important with a crowd of kids following him.

"Can't we see the scar?" Cindy begged.

Ben hung back. Not me, he thought. He'd already seen plenty of scars in comic books—long red lines with little knots tying the two parts together. They looked just like the tops of dogfood bags. Could you undo Boyd's stomach by pulling on the last stitch? he wondered. The thought of little brown lumps spilling out of his wound onto the ground

crowded into Ben's mind and set his stomach bubbling.

Ben stayed away from Boyd until lunch when
he lined up for a tray of hamburger gravy on curly
noodles. "Oo-oh." He took one look at the mound
and asked Mrs. Linden if he could go to the bathroom, but when he pushed open the door Boyd was
in the corner with a group of boys gathered around
him.

"You wanna see, Tyler?" Boyd asked, and the
boys all turned around to look at Ben.

"Um . . . not really." Ben swallowed hard.
Somehow he knew he was going to end up looking
at that scar.

"I'm not doing this again, so you'd better look
now while you have the chance."

Peering between Patrick, Dennis and Lance,
Ben could see the bare skin of Boyd's legs. "That's
okay," he said trying to sound friendly. "I've seen
them in books."

Boyd grinned, showing his dirty teeth. "Well,
nobody leaves without looking. Get him over here,"
Boyd ordered.

A row of wash basins blocked Ben's way to the
door. No escape. I'll just take a quick look and take
off, Ben thought, and slowly moved toward the group
in the corner. Boyd stood with his jeans down around
his bony white knees and the elastic of his shorts

stretched to show a red mark that was not much bigger than a paper clip. There weren't even any stitches showing.

It was so little Ben almost laughed.

"Cool, isn't it?" Boyd asked, twisting his stomach back and forth like a hula dancer. Then he pulled up his pants and buckled them.

Ben wasn't going to tell him his scar wasn't any good, but the truth was, it didn't seem like much, not half as bad as Ben's swollen nose had been. Looks like they just poked a hole to let some of the air out, Ben wanted to say. "Yeah, cool, I guess."

Suddenly Boyd reached out and grabbed Ben's shirt, pushing him backward at the same time. The small of his back rammed into the edge of one of the wash basins.

"You guess?"

Automatically Ben went into the Horse Stance with his fists up. His foot was halfway in the air going toward Boyd's middle when he stopped himself. I could rip everything open again and put him back in the hospital, Ben thought. I could be expelled, or worse. What would Sifu say if I kicked a kid who'd had an operation?

Boyd let go and jumped back. "You're darn lucky you didn't kick me," he growled and put his hand over his scar as if he suddenly figured out what could have happened.

118

Ben straightened himself as he began to shake inside. "I'm not half as lucky as you are," he managed to answer. "If it hadn't been for your scar. . . ."

Ben glanced toward the door expecting to see the principal, or his mother. *If you can't be nice you'll have to come in.* Her angry words came back to him. But I *am* nice, he thought clearly.

"I want to know something, Boyd. Why do you hate me?"

Boyd stared at Ben with his arms hanging loose at his sides. "I don't know," he said. "Just 'cause."

Somehow Ben felt braver than he ever had before. Maybe it was because he knew Boyd couldn't do anything to him, or maybe it was seeing himself in the Horse Stance and remembering the things Sifu had taught him. He wiggled his shoulders and stood as tall as he could, which was the same height as Boyd, and said, "Well, hurry up and get better. Next time I'm gonna smear you."

A hard swallow dropped to the bottom of Ben's throat. Who said that? Lance, Dennis and Patrick started to laugh. Ben's face went hot.

"Ha!" Boyd bellowed. "That'll be the day. In the first place, I won't be around all summer."

"I can wait."

Boyd poked his finger into Ben's chest and left the bathroom with the others following. "See you in sixth grade, if you don't die of fright first."

2

On June sixth school let out for the summer, and Mrs. Linden opened her present, a plastic Kleenex box with apple blossoms glued to the top. She turned it over, examining it with watery eyes.

"I've enjoyed having each and every one of you," she lied. "Good luck to all of you in sixth grade."

Ben said good-bye with a surprising twinge of sadness. Now that the year was over, Mrs. Linden didn't seem so bad.

The bell rang, and the class raced out the door to load the bus for the last time that year.

On the way, Boyd worked a squirt gun out of his pants pocket and aimed it at Michele's new lace dress. Purple splotches of ink popped up all over one side of the long skirt and in little beads on the toes of her shoes.

The door of the bus jerked open, and the driver came rushing out. "Boyd, I've had enough of you!"

Michele held her arms up as if her sleeves were

dripping wet and stared down at her dress. Then she threw her head back and wailed.

Ben watched hopefully as the bus driver opened a notebook and jotted something down, then tore off the page and handed it to Boyd.

"What's this?" Boyd asked, grinning.

"A bad-behavior slip."

It figured, Ben thought. Giving Boyd a bad-behavior slip on the last day of school. It would probably ruin his whole summer. Ha.

Boyd wadded up the note and flicked it at Michele.

Ben sat with Charles on the bus and watched Boyd get off at the apartments. The Bradshaws must have moved while he was in the hospital, Ben decided. Too bad they had to tell him. Oh well, he thought, fall was a long way off and Boyd wouldn't be around all summer.

But the more Ben thought about it, the more certain he was that there wouldn't be another miracle. Sifu was right—Ben was going to have to fight him or be miserable next year, too.

For a minute he was sorry fifth grade was over. Now he would have to worry about Boyd all summer. "Know what, Charles?"

"What?"

"I almost beat up Boyd Bradshaw the other day."

121

Charles looked at him amazed. "You did not."

"Yes, I did. It's true. My foot was in the air and everything. I would have kicked him right in the stomach if it hadn't been for his scar."

"I would have kicked him anyway." The toe of Charles's shoe hit the back of the seat in front of them, then he got up to leave at his stop. Waji peered over the top with her eyebrows pulled low over her eyes. When she saw Ben, her look changed to a smile and she grinned at him for two blocks.

"Hi," Ben said finally.

She stuck out a fat pink tongue. "I hate you."

Good, Ben thought and a few minutes later he jumped from the steps of the bus onto the warm gravel and headed home. His report card was in one hand along with a social studies notebook and some math papers. In the other hand he carried his baseball. He tossed it into the air until it almost disappeared against the blue sky, then caught it again as it dropped neatly into the palm of his hand. Ben smiled a huge smile and broke into a run. The whole summer lay ahead. And Bradshaw had no part in it.

At that moment fall seemed like a long, long time away.

During the next three months Roger and Ben practiced their Sets together, went swimming, taught Daisy how to jump picnic benches and ate dozens of

Popsicles. Sometimes the boys stayed at Roger's house, and other times they stayed at Ben's.

Roger had changed during his month at kajukenbo, and Ben now saw clearly that they were more alike than different. At least Roger was one person who understood Ben's feelings about fighting, and kajukenbo was something they had in common.

One sweaty day in July, as they were doing their Sets outside the kajukenbo school in the parking lot, Sifu asked if they wanted to try for their belts. Roger still did not have his yellow, and Ben was working on an orange.

"I'm not ready." Roger's eyes widened and his whole body seemed to sink backward.

"Try, and we'll see." The soft steady voice left no way for Roger to say he couldn't do it.

"Don't worry," Ben whispered. "Sifu knows when you're ready."

Roger was required to do two minutes in the Horse Stance and Ben had to do four, plus nine basic Sets, three Concentrations and three Monkey Forms.

Ben had already done four minutes in the Horse Stance, by mistake the first time Roger had timed him, so he knew he could do it, and he wasn't at all surprised when Sifu tossed him an orange belt all folded up in a paper band.

Roger unfolded his yellow belt. "Gosh," he

123

said. "I never thought I'd get one of these."

"You've come a long way," Sifu said. "Do you still want to quit?"

Roger turned even redder than he already was from the hot sun. "How did you know?"

"I size people up quickly." Sifu smiled. "Those who are here for the wrong reason usually don't stick it out very long."

The boys looked at each other, and Ben knew his friend was thinking the same thing he was—they would be here until they were grown-ups if they had to, but they were going all the way to Black Belt. Both he and Roger had come a long way.

Suddenly one day Ben realized that summer was almost over. He went into Jill's room to get her out of bed. She raised up on one elbow and blinked at him.

"Wake up," he said sliding into a Horse Stance and flinging a few punches into the air. "Mom says we have to go shopping for school clothes."

Jill's hair was all pushed up on one side where she had been sleeping, and her left cheek was covered with red lines.

"What are you doing?" she mumbled.

"Nothing. You have to get up." Ben turned sideways and shot a kick toward the top ruffle on her canopy bed.

124

"I mean . . . that. What are you doing?" She reached for her window shade and let it roll with a flap, flap, flap around the rod at the top.

Ben looked down at his fists. "You mean this? It's kajukenbo."

"You're nuts, Benny, you know that? Every time I look at you lately you're jumping around like some sort of wild man. Can't you practice somewhere else?" Jill yawned so wide Ben could see the little thing hanging down in the back of her throat.

"I'm not practicing . . . exactly."

"Well, if you're going to punch something, punch Boyd Bradshaw."

Ben stopped where he was. "What'd you have to mention him for?"

"You aren't still worried about that creep, are you? If he gets near you, you're liable to knock him out without even knowing it." Jill put her robe on and crossed in front of Ben to her mirror.

His arms had started flying around again as if they had separate brains of their own.

"Stoppit!" she hollered and ducked as Ben's fist flew past her nose. "Benny, you're driving me crazy. Mo-om?" Jill padded through the doorway in her slippers. "Does he have to go with us?"

The Tylers went school shopping, and Ben got three new pairs of jeans and some really great shirts, a bunch of socks, two pairs of shoes and some under-wear in plastic packages; he lined everything up in his drawers and waited for school to start again.

The following Tuesday Mrs. Tyler dropped Jill off at the junior high and drove Ben on to Hilltop. Groups of kids crowded around the windows of the principal's office where lists of room assignments were taped.

"Do you want me to come in with you?" Mom asked.

"No, thanks. I can do it." Ben turned around and looked at the front of the building. It seemed as if he'd just been there yesterday. Kids ran like bugs all over the playground, screaming and laughing. What were they so happy about? Ben's stomach crawled toward his throat. I'm not ready, he wanted to scream.

Ben's promise to Boyd stuck in his mind—*I'm gonna smear you*. Maybe he's forgotten, Ben thought. Maybe . . . nothing. I'm not going to get another miracle. I've already had three when most people don't even get one.

Ben said good-bye to his mother as slowly as he could and headed into the school. Where will I be tomorrow? he wondered. What will my nose look like?

22

Ben crowded up to the lists between Mike Sanford and Celia and ran his finger down the pages until he found Tyler, Benjamin. The teacher's name at the top was Mrs. Sandhurst, someone new.

Please save me one more time, he prayed to the ceiling. I'll get straight A's for the rest of my life and never say a bad word. Ben's eyes continued down the list to the last name, added in pencil. Boyd Bradshaw.

It figures, Ben thought, and he looked over his shoulder to see if anyone was watching; then he slipped his new pink eraser out of his pocket and smudged away the name. It wouldn't really do any good, he knew, but he smiled to himself before he walked down the green hallway toward his new classroom. Maybe Mrs. Sandhurst would be a tough teacher who wouldn't let Boyd get away with anything.

Ben checked the doors all the way down the hall to Room Twenty-three and peeked in. Cindy, in a new curly hairdo, stood sharpening pencils.

127

Lance was wearing glasses. Everyone looked different with stiff new clothes and haircuts. A boy Ben didn't know sat alone near the windows looking up at the faces moving around the room.

Ben waited outside the door to take several long breaths. Everyone had changed. Maybe Boyd had changed too. After being away all summer, he could be a completely new person.

Then he heard a roar coming from down the hall and the loud stomp of running footsteps. He turned to see Boyd and two other kids dribbling a basketball between them toward Room Twenty-three. They crashed past Ben into the classroom.

Boyd's blond hair stuck out in all directions like straw, and the jeans he wore had no color at all, as if he'd worn the same pair all summer. Shoelaces flew from both feet.

"Hey, Tyler. You ready for our fight?" Boyd knocked a chair over on his way to the coatroom. He hadn't changed a bit.

Ben thought fast. "There's a new rule," he said. "No fighting." He was in school again, and all his problems were starting over. Ben's hand went to his stomach.

"Boys! That'll be enough! Put the ball away and take your seats."

A happy smile covered Ben's entire face as he stepped into the room to look toward the teacher's desk. He knew that voice! Could it really be. . . .

"Miss Fletcher! Are you substituting already?"

Her blue-green eyes twinkled as she looked at Ben. "I'm not substituting and I'm not Miss Fletcher anymore. I got *married* this summer."

She said the word "married" as if it were the greatest thing that had ever happened to her.

"Oh, you did?" Don't sound sad, Ben told himself. After all, she couldn't marry someone who's only eleven. "You mean you're going to be our regular teacher?"

"That's right."

Michele entered the room. "Oh, hi, Miss Fletcher."

"You're all going to have to get used to calling me Mrs. Sandhurst. I'm married now."

Michele clasped her hands together. "Oh, that's neat," she said.

I may call her Mrs. Sandhurst out loud, Ben thought, but inside she's still Miss Fletcher.

"Guess who's back?" Shelley asked a group of kids coming in the door. "The substitute." Then the teacher explained about her marriage all over again.

As she talked, Boyd sat quietly at a desk in the back of the room, and the ache faded away from Ben's stomach. He was safe in the room with Miss Fletcher, he figured.

The first thing she did when the bell rang was

make out a seating chart, with Boyd in the front next to her desk. Girls sat on all sides of him. Ben turned his head toward the windows and smiled.

"I'm not going to sit here all year," Boyd complained. "It's not fair."

"I'll be reassigning seats at the beginning of every month," she said. "Boyd, if you can behave until the first of October, you may sit somewhere else."

"A whole month?" he whined.

Forget it Bradshaw, Ben wanted to say, you'll be sitting there all year.

Miss Fletcher assigned Ben to the second seat next to the window, behind the new kid and across from Craig Olsen. Everyone seemed happy except Boyd, who slumped down in his seat and pouted all morning.

At recess Ben stayed in to help the teacher pass out spelling books. He hated Boyd and now he hated himself, too, for staying inside. Where was the courage Sifu had promised?

"I see nothing has changed between you and Boyd," Miss Fletcher said when they were finished. "I'm sorry."

"I'm still taking kajukenbo lessons," Ben told her. "I'll be getting my purple belt pretty soon."

"Good for you, Ben." She smiled down at him. "I'll bet you're a real tiger."

130

"Not exactly." The snarling tiger from the painting at kajukenbo popped into Ben's mind. "I'm not sure it's doing any good. I still haven't had a fight. I'm more like a kitten." He tried to laugh.

"Have you changed your mind? Do you want to fight?"

"No, but I told Boyd I'd fight him when school started."

"Oh, dear." Miss Fletcher frowned.

"I don't know why I said I would. It's the dumbest thing I've ever done."

Ben glanced toward the windows to see Boyd's nose flattened against the glass like a pig.

"Come on out, Tyler." Lance and Patrick stood behind Boyd, smiling and beckoning.

"I have to get these spelling books passed out," Ben hollered through the glass. "It'll probably take all recess." He looked sheepishly at Miss Fletcher. "They probably want me to play baseball," he said.

Boyd and the others flapped their elbows up and down and made chicken noises.

Ben's insides moved like a mound of fishing worms. Do something, he commanded himself, but his feet seemed glued to the ground.

After school Ben hurried out the door. His problems were worse than ever. He still didn't want to fight, but neither did he want to come to school feeling the same awful way tomorrow.

As he stood fidgeting in the bus line, Ben wondered if he should just walk up to Boyd and punch him in the nose, get it over with once and for all? Maybe Boyd would pass out right away and wouldn't even try to hit back.

Before Ben could decide on a plan, Boyd crowded in behind him and stuffed a wad of dusty pine needles down his shirt. Ben's stomach flopped upside down, and his chest began to thud. He needed one more lesson with Sifu, then he could clobber Boyd for sure. Tomorrow, not today.

"Knock it off, Boyd. I've just about had it."

"Good," Boyd breathed into Ben's ear.

Turnips. Where does he get all those turnips? Ben wondered. "We aren't supposed to fight on the school grounds," he said, trying to keep his voice from shaking. His hand covered his nose as if he knew what was coming.

Just then a car horn blasted, and Ben looked up to see the Tylers' station wagon pull into the parking lot. Daisy bounced in the front seat. His mother stopped near the bus and pushed the door open. "Get in," she called.

Ben let out the breath that he didn't know he was holding. "Thank you," he whispered, looking toward the sky. Relief washed over him like cool

132

water from a hose. He could worry about tomorrow later.

Daisy bounced off the seat and out onto the gravel. "Hi, Daisy," Ben hollered and slapped his knees so she'd come to him. Her ears flopped and her legs crisscrossed as she raced toward Ben as fast as she could.

"Gees, what an ugly dog," Boyd growled.

Ben ignored him and reached out his arms for Daisy as Boyd's foot flew up and caught the dog in the stomach.

Daisy screeched, rolled over twice, then lay still near a pile of pine needles. Ben stood numb, looking down at the gray hump. Mrs. Tyler stumbled out of the car and started toward Daisy. Miss Fletcher hollered something behind Ben, but he wasn't listening.

Ben looked into Boyd's face, at his skinny long nose and yellow teeth, and something went crazy inside of him. In one second everything Sifu had said replayed itself like a tape recording. *Someday someone will make you angry enough . . . you don't have to beat a bully. . . .* Without even thinking his hands went into position and his knees bent in the Horse Stance. The proud grin on Boyd's face slipped into a white scowl, as if he knew he'd finally gone too far.

133

23

Blood pulsed in Ben's ears so that he could hardly hear.

"Look what you've done to my dog!" Hot tears streamed down his cheeks and his throat seemed to close as his fist struck Boyd's chin. Boyd gasped, and his head snapped back.

Ben glanced anxiously at Daisy lying on the ground with his mother and Miss Fletcher bent over her. His chest pounded wildly as he flew at Boyd. Ben knew he couldn't stop himself now.

He wheeled around and shot the side of his left foot into Boyd's stomach. As Boyd doubled over kids screamed, "Get him, Ben! Cream him!"

Ben slid forward into the Horse Stance and crashed into the side of Boyd's face with the palm of his left hand, then moved in behind Boyd and hooked his right leg to jerk him off balance. Boyd reeled backward groaning. Kids ran from their places in the bus lines to cheer Ben on.

Just then, it wasn't Ben who was fighting. Some-

thing inside worked his body as if it were a machine. "Come on, Ben. You can do it!" Was that Miss Fletcher?

Boyd pulled himself to his knees and tried to stand up. "Tyler, you've had—"

Ben pushed at Boyd's shoulder with his foot and knocked him down again. It all seemed so easy.

"Leave me alone," Boyd cried. A howl of laughter followed from the crowd of kids.

All Ben could think of was his dog. He turned his back and ran to the woolly gray hump cradled in his mother's lap. As he looked down, Daisy's brown eyes rolled toward him, and her tail thumped against Mrs. Tyler's knee. At least she was still alive.

Suddenly Patrick screamed, "Look out, Benjamin!"

Boyd's weight landed on Ben's back, and his arms locked around his chest. The air rushed out of his lungs like a squashed balloon.

"That's enough! Stop it!" Mrs. Tyler ordered them. "Fighting doesn't solve anything!"

Mom was standing up holding Daisy, and her face was greenish-white, as if she were going to be sick. Ben heard her words, but this time he knew Boyd had to give up first.

Ben jabbed backward with his elbow and caught Boyd in the ribs. Boyd's arms fell away as he grabbed his side. Then Ben wheeled around and twisted

Boyd's arm until he fell to his knees.

"Give it up," Ben said, surprising himself.

"My arm!" Boyd screamed. "Let go!"

Ben's grip loosened, and Boyd jumped up to renew the fight. Without thinking Ben blocked with his left arm, then drove his fist forward to connect with Boyd's mouth. Ben cringed as teeth splintered behind his knuckles.

Surprise spread across Boyd's face, then finally he crumpled over. Ben waited, ready for him to jump up again, but this time Boyd did not move.

He made me do it, Ben thought, unable to understand or to believe it. Boyd *wanted* to fight.

Kids yelled and cheered from all sides. Ben noticed Patrick and Celia and Waji. Charles stood by a tree grinning. What were they so happy about? That Boyd lost? or that Ben had won?

Mrs. Tyler appeared behind him with Daisy in her arms.

Ben breathed hard. "I couldn't help it, Mom. I tried not to fight, but I had to."

"I know," she said, touching his shoulder. They both looked down at Boyd.

Blood trickled from the corner of his mouth. Dark red rivers, like fake vampire blood, ran down and dripped off his chin. Boyd lay there with his face to the sun, his eyelids twitching as if he were trying to wake up.

137

"Oh, my gosh. Look what I've done!" Ben's stomach jerked, and he passed the principal as he ran into the school building, down the hall and straight to the boys' bathroom. Would he make it in time? Ben's stomach heaved in and out.

He leaned on the basin as he tried to figure it all out. It was as if he had passed through a doorway into some terrible place where people beat on each other for the fun of it, a place he could never return from. Daisy was hurt, and part of Ben wanted to pummel Boyd until there was nothing left. The other part of him was back in the sandbox. What he had done to Boyd was not "nice," but he could never undo it now. Why had Boyd picked on him in the first place and made Ben do this horrible thing?

I must have knocked all his teeth out, Ben thought. I'll be expelled. His parents will make me pay to have his teeth put back in.

Ben checked his own white face in the mirror. He expected to see blood on himself too, but he was not even scratched. Boyd looked much worse than he did.

While he stood there leaning over the basin, the principal, Mr. Parker, came in with Boyd, who held his hand over his mouth. Blood splotched the front of the boy's shirt.

Boyd pulled down a handful of paper towels, wet them under the faucet and packed them against

138

his jaw. Then he sat down on a bench and leaned against the wall with his eyes closed. Ben tried to see if any teeth were missing.

"What's going on, boys?"

"Well . . ." Ben began to explain.

"He started it," Boyd whined. "I never even touched him."

24

Mr. Parker looked from one boy to the other. "I find that very hard to believe, Boyd, after all the trouble you've been in."

Boyd turned the paper towels over and pressed the cool side to his chin. "Look what he did to me," he complained.

Ben stiffened. "Shut up, Boyd!" he said right out loud. "You nearly killed my dog. You had it coming."

"If there are vet bills to pay," Mr. Parker told Ben, "let me know and I'll talk to Mrs. Bradshaw."

Boyd glared as if the whole thing were Ben's fault, but he didn't say another word until they were following Mr. Parker to the parking lot.

"My mom's not paying for anything," Boyd said under his breath. "I'll tell her I didn't do it."

"The whole school saw you," Ben said more calmly now.

"You think you're pretty smart, don't you?

140

Does that karate stuff work against five or six guys at once?"

"A hundred," Ben said and swallowed hard. Sometimes, it doesn't even work against one, he thought grimly.

Boyd looked at him as if he weren't sure whether to believe it or not. "You're lying," he said, "aren't you?"

Ben didn't answer.

"AREN'T YOU? Well, it doesn't matter anyway. We'll get you one way or another."

Mr. Parker turned around. "There'll be no more fighting on the school grounds. You're lucky you weren't hurt worse, Boyd."

Ben's mother and Miss Fletcher were waiting anxiously in the parking lot.

"Are you all right, son."

"Yeah, I'm okay now."

"What about me?" Boyd said. "I'm the one who's really hurt." He pushed on one of his front teeth. "My mom is probably gonna sue."

"I'm going to call your mother this afternoon," Miss Fletcher said in an angry voice. "I'm sure she'll want to know how this really happened."

Mrs. Tyler drove Daisy to the pet hospital and skipped kajukenbo, but Ben didn't mind. He was too upset to concentrate anyway.

The doctor wrapped a bandage around Daisy's chest and gave her some pills. "She'll be fine in a few days," he said. "Her ribs are just bruised."

Ben held her on his lap all the way home and let her sleep that night with her head on his pillow. She looked real peaceful, he thought, with the sheet tucked under her chin and one paw sticking out.

"You dumb dog. Why did you have to jump out of the car? Don't you ever do that again," he scolded, and Daisy's tail wagged under the covers. Most of the night Ben lay awake watching Daisy sleep while he relived his fight with Boyd.

The strange feeling of his own knuckles crashing into Boyd's teeth set Ben twitching. Sifu had known all along that he could fight if he had to, he thought. Could he have fought Boyd that first time at the bus stop? he wondered. Could he have done it without the lessons? He'd never know for sure.

Ben turned over twice and rearranged his blankets. If he had to fight again for something important, he guessed he could. But he hoped nothing important would come up again for a long time.

Hours later, in the middle of the night, Ben finally fell asleep with one arm draped over Daisy.

The next morning Dad grinned at Ben across the table. "Well, Benny, looks as if you've solved your problem. That Bradshaw kid will leave you alone from now on. What do you think of kajukenbo now?"

How could Ben tell his father that he hated the idea of fighting just as much as before?

"I almost knocked Boyd's teeth out," Ben said. "I could have broken his arm."

Jill pulled her head out of the refrigerator where she was searching for some jam. "Why didn't you? The creep had it coming."

"I don't know why."

"You're impossible, you know that, Benny?" Jill said.

Dad put his hand on Ben's shoulder. "You see, Ann. I told you our boy wouldn't turn into a bully. Being a bully is all in the mind, not the fist. I like you just the way you are, son."

Ben yawned and smiled. After his night with Daisy, all he wanted to do was go to sleep, but it was another school day, and half an hour later he climbed reluctantly onto the bus again.

Patrick scooted toward the window. "I saved you a seat," he said.

What was going on?

"No thanks," he told Patrick. "I already promised someone else," and he slid into an empty seat, waiting for Charles.

"Hey, Benjamin," Charles called, getting on at

the next stop. "You really did it. You wiped out Boyd Bradshaw. Do you think you could teach me to do that?"

"I don't know. It takes a long time. Anyway, maybe you already know how and you just don't know it."

"Huh?"

"Oh, never mind."

"We're still best friends, aren't we, Benjamin?" Charles's blue eyes widened.

"Sure."

When they got to Boyd's stop, Ben wasn't the only one looking out for his old enemy. The whole bus was waiting for him. But Boyd wasn't there. Had his jaw swollen and turned purple like Ben's nose?

All the rest of the way to school Ben listened to stories about himself and Boyd. Celia, who had called him a wimp, said he could probably smear anyone in sixth grade.

Leave me alone, Ben wanted to scream at her. Don't expect me to fight anyone else. I'm no different than I was before.

"Not everyone," Craig argued.

"He could too, couldn't you, Benjamin?" Celia insisted.

"My name's not Benjamin. It's Ben," he said and looked out the window to watch the trees and houses moving past. His head bumped against the

144

glass, and his eyelids drooped. Daisy would have to sleep in her own bed tonight, he thought, yawning again.

Lance startled him a few minutes later when he howled and jerked the window down. "There's Boyd!" he yelled. "Hey, Bradshaw, what's the matter? You scared to ride the bus?"

The kids turned to stare, and to laugh at Boyd, who rode along the shoulder on a red bike.

Ben was glad that for once he was not the one they were teasing, but he squirmed in his seat just the same.

25

Sifu sat cross-legged on the mat with his eyes closed. "How did you feel, Ben," he asked quietly, "when you confronted your enemy?"

Ben watched Sifu's face with the locked eyelashes and freckles on his cheeks. He looked like a regular man, but Ben knew he wasn't.

"I didn't feel scared or sick or anything . . . until later." Ben leaned against the wall and stretched out his legs.

"Did you survive?" Sifu smiled and opened his eyes.

"Well . . . yes, but. . . ."

"But you didn't like the way you felt?"

"No. I still hate fighting."

Sifu draped his arms over his knees. "It's okay to be Ben Tyler," he said. "How do you feel right now?"

That was a hard question. He felt a lot of ways. "Boyd says he's going to get his friends together and

146

beat me up again. I think he *likes* to fight."

"You only had to prove you could win once. Some people have to prove it over and over again."

Ben turned and looked at Sifu. "I'm sure glad I'm not like that. But what can I do? Won't I have to defend myself? This could go on forever."

"You'll know what to do," Sifu said.

"There's one other thing I've been wondering about."

"What's that?"

Ben was almost afraid to ask. "What if Boyd decides to take lessons, too? How can I defend myself if he knows the same tricks?"

Sifu smiled and touched Ben's shoulder. "He'll have to attack you first, and you already know a number of ways to block him. If he's really interested in learning kajukenbo, tell him to give me a call. Maybe we can teach him a better attitude. But I don't think you have to worry, Ben."

Good, Ben thought. "Why not?"

"He would have to learn to salute me and to endure the Horse Stance. He would have to be here almost every day. Do you think he would be willing to work that hard?"

That's just what Mike had said about Warren Bogel, Ben remembered, and he realized suddenly that Warren had disappeared after the first few days.

147

Ben had not even noticed when he quit. He tried to picture Boyd in the Horse Stance with sweat dripping off his forehead.

"He probably would rather just learn the Sets," Ben admitted.

"Remember when I told you there were two parts to kajukenbo? The part in your fist and the part in your mind?"

"Yeah."

"A bully often picks on other kids because he's afraid."

"Boyd afraid? He's not afraid of anything."

Sifu stood up and settled into the Horse Stance. Ben did the same.

"He may not be afraid of fighting, but maybe he's afraid of looking stupid. Maybe he's afraid of math problems or spelling tests."

"You're right! It's fractions. He can't figure them out." Ben struck toward the mirror with his fists. He liked the way his muscles seemed to know what to do.

"Well, Ben, if he shows up here maybe kajukenbo can turn him around and teach him not to be afraid."

Greg came in to salute then, and Sifu left Ben to help him with a new Set.

Fractions, Ben thought. So that's it. Boyd hates me because I can do fractions and he can't. I wonder why he doesn't pick on Patrick? Patrick can do fractions, too.

Boyd was still a puzzle, but Ben felt less confused than he had been before. Sifu is really smart, he thought. I'll bet if he were the President of the World, there wouldn't be any wars.

Sifu approached Ben again later. "By the way," he said, "there's going to be a belt promotion next month. I think you're almost ready to try for your purple belt."

"Because of the fight?" Ben asked surprised.

"Of course not. Because you will have learned the required Sets and Concentrations."

"That's great!" Ben's entire body smiled. This time the belt would not merely be thrown to him. He would be tested with the other men and receive his purple belt in a real ceremony . . . if he made it.

A month seemed like a long time to wait, but Ben needed the time to get ready.

The days until the promotion crawled by slowly, but at least school was not miserable anymore. The day after Ben talked to Sifu, Boyd swaggered out onto the playground.

"All right," he announced in his usual way, "I'm captain. Follow me."

Patrick stopped dead in his tracks. "Wait a minute! Who says?"

Red-faced, Boyd stepped close to him and yelled in his face, "I says."

"Maybe we'd rather have Ben Tyler for captain," Patrick persisted bravely. "At least he knows how to play baseball."

"Yeah," said Lance, "You want to be captain, Ben?"

"Sure. I guess so."

Boyd opened his mouth, but nothing came out. He shrunk back. "I'm not playing with that creep," he said. "Count me out." He waited for someone to stop him, but no one did.

"That's all right with me," Boyd said finally. "I'm getting sick of baseball anyway."

Ben watched him slink away from the group. This wasn't the way it was supposed to turn out. After the fight, Boyd was supposed to apologize and promise never to be mean again. Instead, he leaned against the maple tree on the playground and spit at Ben when he passed.

"What's the matter?" Boyd grumbled one day, "you afraid of a rematch? You know I could smear you any day of the week, don't you?"

"Any day except Tuesday," Ben said, and Boyd threw his whole body into a spit that landed near Ben's shoe.

"Hey, Boyd. Why don't we call off this feud? I never wanted to fight with you anyway. Maybe I can help you with your fractions."

"What's *that* got to do with anything? You're crazy, Tyler."

Finally the month passed, and before Ben could work up a good stomachache, it was the night before the belt promotion.

Mom, Dad and Jill came into his room with a big box. Ben's sister smiled like a crocodile. "Remember, kajukenbo was all my idea in the first place," she bragged.

"Sifu said it would be nice if you had this," his mother told him as she held out the box.

Ben knew what it was, but he pretended to be surprised when he lifted the lid and saw the black cloth. He pulled out a jacket, just his size, and a pair of trousers with laces in the front.

Pictures swirled in Ben's mind of himself in midair kicking with the sides of his feet and of himself in the Horse Stance with his fists at his sides.

"Gosh, this is great," Ben said. "Thanks everybody."

"Try them on," his father urged. "Let's see how you look."

Ben slipped into the new outfit and tied his orange belt around his waist, then stood in front of a long mirror. "I used to think these outfits looked like pajamas." He laughed. "But not any more."

"Oh, he's so cute," Mrs. Tyler said.

Dad scowled at her and said, "Tomorrow you can trade that orange belt for a purple."

"If I make it," Ben reminded him.

"You'll make it all right, Benny," Jill said. "I know you will."

Ben looked at her puzzled. Wasn't she the one who had said he was driving her crazy? "But, what if I don't?"

Dad put his arm around Ben. "If you don't make it, you can try again next time. The main thing is that you're nobody's pushover anymore, and it doesn't matter what kind of belt you're wearing."

Ben felt proud in his new outfit when his father dropped him off the next morning.

"Good luck, Ben. I know you can do it."

"I hope so," Ben said, and wiped his sweaty hands on the legs of his trousers. "Um . . . see you tonight at the ceremony."

Mike arrived at the same time to try for his brown belt, which was next to the highest. Ben braced himself to be lifted up as usual, but Mike shook his hand. "Hi, kid. So you're going to be one of the men. Do you think you'll make it?"

"I don't know. Sifu thinks I'm ready."

Mike punched at him a couple of times. "Yeah, I think so, too. I wish I could have taken lessons when I was eleven."

152

About sixteen men showed up, some of them Ben had never met. They hopped around nervously and hit their fists against the palms of their hands waiting for Sifu.

Finally, he entered with two men who were instructors from other kajukenbo schools. Sifu explained that the three of them would be judges. Everyone saluted and the trials began.

Ben looked up at Mike. He did not think about Boyd or worry about fighting. There was only room in his brain for kajukenbo and concentrating on his purple belt. This is it, he thought. The real thing.

26

First, one of the instructors passed out written tests. The students sat on the floor and answered questions about the founder of the system of kajukenbo, the emerging center and other facts that Sifu had taught them.

Ben's test was only two pages long, so he finished early and looked around the gym. Seven of the men wore orange belts like his and would be going for purple.

"Time's up," Sifu said in his usual soft voice. "Turn in your tests and form a circle in the center of the room." Everyone seemed to know what was going on but Ben.

"We'll start with the highest belt here," Sifu explained. "Mike, that will be you, trying for your brown belt. You'll do thirty minutes in the Horse Stance."

Mike nodded.

"I'll tell each group when to begin, so you can all end up together."

154

Mike lowered himself into the Horse Stance and Ben's chest began to pound. No one could do thirty minutes, could they? That was half an hour! Quickly Ben subtracted in his head. Purple belts were required to do seven minutes, so Ben would not have to begin for twenty-three minutes.

The room was silent except for feet moving around. Ben concentrated on the floor and waited for the clock to move. After a short time the sound of Mike's heavy breathing drowned out everything else.

At twenty-five minutes those going for Green Belts settled into position and started the Horse Stance. Mike's knees began to shake and sweat rolled off his forehead.

Ben felt sick inside. It seemed as if Mike would not be able to finish. Several minutes went by. Ben heard a whimper and looked across the circle to see that one of the Green Belts was already having trouble. His legs buckled under him and he fell backward, then pulled himself up again.

Mike threw his head back and closed his eyes. All Ben could see was his neck and fuzzy beard. At fourteen minutes Blue Belts began.

"Seven minutes," Sifu announced at last. "Those trying for Purple Belts please begin."

That's me, Ben thought, and he sank down, feeling the pull across the tops of his legs. He doubled his fists at his waist. Time ticked away slowly. Everyone in the circle was in the Horse Stance now, and half of the men were shaking.

How can I do it if they can't? Ben wondered. I'm only eleven. Will Sifu understand if I quit? Just stand up and walk away?

The sound of heavy breathing filled the room, and the air became damp and hot. Ben closed his eyes when he started to shake and imagined himself running along the beach with Daisy.

The man opposite Ben collapsed again. "Get up," Sifu ordered him. "Tough it out."

Let him stop! This is crazy, Ben thought. His own legs quivered, but something would not let him quit. Maybe it was Mike, standing trancelike in the center of the circle, going for thirty minutes. Ben looked into the eyes of the dragon on the wall as it watched all of them struggling.

"I'm going to make it," Ben told the beast quietly.

Then a strange thing happened. "Okay. That's it," Sifu said. "Time." But instead of groaning or falling on the floor as they wanted to, every man in the room, including Ben, stood up. Knowing that he had survived seven minutes in the Horse Stance along with the other men filled Ben with pride.

Sometimes hurting can feel good, Ben decided, like wiggling a loose tooth. Maybe that's what Sifu meant when he said, "Make friends with pain."

156

The third part of the test involved ordinary sit-ups. The last ten of Ben's required one hundred pulled so hard at his stomach that he thought his muscles would rip loose, but somehow he got through them and went out into the parking lot where they all loaded into cars.

"Where are we going?"

"Climb in," Mike said. "You can ride with me. We're going over to the track to run our laps. This part will be easy for you, kid."

Mike was right. Ben ran his laps easily and sat on the grass to watch the others finish up. By then it was nearly noon, and Sifu and most of the other men decided to go to a Mexican restaurant for lunch. Ben's mother had packed him a sack lunch, which he figured he'd eat back in the gym.

Mike approached him smiling. "Looks like we're doing okay so far, kid. I just saw the scores."

"Really?" Ben brightened. "Are you sure?"

"Of course, I'm sure. Hey, why don't you and I get some hamburgers. I can't hack that Mexican stuff." Mike rubbed his stomach and pretended to be sick. "It's on me."

"That sounds a lot better than peanut butter. Okay."

Mike drove his old blue car to a little restaurant nearby and passed the drive-up window to park in the rear.

157

Next to them, on the opposite side of the car, Ben noticed two guys in dirty undershirts just getting out of a brand new pick-up truck.

"I'm famished," Mike said, pushing open his door at exactly the same time the pick-up door opened. Metal crunched against metal, and Ben winced as the pair piled out of the truck. One was a rough-looking man of about twenty-five with cigarettes rolled into the sleeve of his undershirt. The other had curly hair and a round belly that hung over his belt buckle.

"Hey, mac," one of them shouted into Mike's face. "Watch what you're doing!"

27

"Sorry about that," Mike said calmly. "Looks like we both did some damage."

Ben's pulse quickened, but he wasn't sure why. If anything happened, Mike could flatten them both in thirty seconds. It wasn't as if it were Ben facing Boyd Bradshaw.

Suddenly the curly-haired one reached right into the window for Mike's shirt and, before Ben could figure out how he did it, Mike was outside of the car with his door shut. Ben scrambled out his side and stood waiting, praying nothing more would happen.

The two from the truck looked a little surprised, but the one with the cigarettes stepped up and said, "Hey, jerk, I don't like your attitude! Looks to me like you did around fifty dollars damage, and I aim to collect—right here!"

What would Mike do? Ben wondered. Use a double kick? or a series of punches? What would Ben do if it were he?

159

Mike seemed perfectly calm. "Wait a minute," he said. "You've done equal damage to my car."

"That beater?" the curly-haired one started in, and he drove his fist into the side of Mike's car, leaving an apple-sized dent.

Ben waited with apprehension as he checked to see if anyone else noticed. There was no Miss Fletcher here. Maybe the restaurant manager would come out and stop them.

"Let's settle it right here," curly challenged.

Here it comes, Ben thought, and he pulled his shoulders in a little.

Mike touched the new dent in his car. "I'd rather settle it peacefully if you don't mind," he said.

"What's the matter? You afraid of getting hurt?"

Ben couldn't believe it. This idiot sounded just like a fifth-grader!

"Yes, I'm afraid of getting hurt," Mike said and stuffed his hands casually into his pockets.

The two looked at each other and snickered.

"Look fellas," Mike said. "You don't know anything about *me,* but I can see that neither of you is in very good shape. One of you is overweight, and the other smokes. Odds are I can beat both of you. Do you want to take a chance?"

Ben looked anxiously from one face to the other during the long silence that followed. Finally the fat

160

one said, "Oh, shoot, Carl, let's go in and eat. It's just a little scratch." And after a grumble and a scowl, the other one followed him into the restaurant.

Mike motioned to Ben. "I'm starved," he said. "How about a hamburger and some fries?"

"In there?" Ben asked. Somehow he had expected that they would get in the car and go somewhere more friendly.

Mike looked surprised. "Of course," he said. "This is a public place, and they make great burgers."

While Ben ate, he glanced more than once at the two men, who were in a booth on the other side of the restaurant. Mike paid no attention to them.

That's how I want to be, Ben thought. I want to be able to ride the bus or eat lunch without even thinking about Boyd Bradshaw.

"Do you think they'll start anything when we leave?" Ben asked.

"Who, them? I hope not!"

"How come?"

"Someone will get hurt. Maybe even me."

Ben laughed. "I know you could beat both of them at once if you wanted to."

Mike leaned toward Ben and whispered. "That's what we made them believe, anyway, huh, kid."

After lunch the judges watched the students, one by one, do their Sets and Concentrations. Roger showed up to be Ben's "dummy" since no one else was his size. They sat cross-legged against the wall and watched each person, starting with the seven who were trying for purple belts.

When it was Ben's turn, he saluted Sifu and started the moves he'd learned, sliding from the Horse Stance into kicks, blocks or punches.

Later, Roger walked out on the floor with Ben and together they did the first fifteen Sets. After each one Roger fell to the floor as if Ben had really beaten him.

Everyone sat quietly and watched the trials for over three and a half hours, then the students lined up and saluted Sifu and the other judges again. Ben's heart pounded, and he let his arm touch Mike as he stood next to him.

"You are all promoted." Sifu smiled as if it were he getting a new belt. He knew all along we would make it, Ben thought, and he stood at attention wondering why no one said a word or even smiled. There were still a lot of things he didn't understand about kajukenbo.

Can't I laugh or yell or anything? he wondered. He stood still and serious like everyone else, but inside he screamed, Hooray! I made it! Ben Tyler is a Purple Belt!

28

Sifu knelt behind a long row of candles in a black silk uniform. Dragons and other designs were stitched to the sleeves and jacket front. A black belt hung from his waist.

Ben stared. He'd never seen a black belt before. It was only made of cloth like the others, but it was different because of what it meant.

Separate candles glowed in front of each student facing Sifu. Ben looked down the row at Mike, who's beard split into a smile when their eyes met.

Behind them in the dark on fold-up chairs sat the families and friends. Roger sat with Mr. and Mrs. Tyler and Jill. Miss Fletcher beamed at Ben from the back row.

Pride swelled in his chest until Ben thought his jacket would pull open.

The first man in line moved up the row of candles to kneel in front of Sifu. This is the best part, Ben thought, when you know you've already made it and all you have to do is sit quietly and feel proud inside.

Ben took his turn and walked down the row of candles, then knelt on the floor. Sifu looked like a stranger, Ben thought, with his face lit up in the dark.

"By the power entrusted to me by my Sifu, Sigung Antonio Romos and by his Sifu, Sijo Adriano Emperado, I promote you to Purple Belt." He held up the folded cloth in front of Ben and snapped the paper band.

"This is a special victory for you, Ben," Sifu said. "You now have a weapon. Use it wisely."

"I will," Ben heard himself squeak, and he tied the stiff purple belt twice around his waist in place of the old orange one. Then he shook hands with Sifu and accepted the certificate rolled up and tied with a black ribbon.

As soon as Mike received his brown belt, the ceremony was over. Someone snapped on the lights, and the word "congratulations" bounced around the room like dozens of flash bulbs going off.

"Let's see your belt," Jill said. "Don't worry. I'm not going to wear it."

Mrs. Tyler hugged Ben. "I guess your dad was right—this once. You're still the same son I had before." Her eyes were beginning to water again, and Ben turned to Miss Fletcher who was saying something to him from his other side.

164

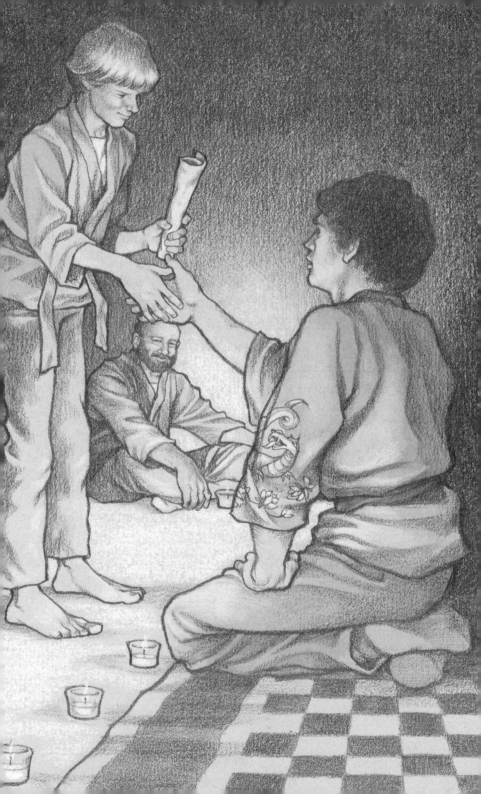

Dad looked at Ben with pride in his eyes. Roger shook his hand and examined the purple belt.

"Next comes blue," Ben told him and unrolled the certificate Sifu had given him. The boys looked at it together. Underneath some fancy Chinese letters, the thin paper was signed by a Phillip Reynolds, Fourth Degree Black Belt.

"Who's he?" Roger asked.

Ben looked through the crowd for Sifu, who stood laughing with one of the relatives in his shiny black uniform. "Phillip Reynolds?" Ben whispered. "So he does have a regular name."

It was just like Miss Fletcher getting married and changing her name to Sandhurst. To Ben she would always be Miss Fletcher, and in the same way Sifu would always be Sifu no matter what his real name was.

At school on Monday Ben felt great. He didn't tell anyone about the belt except Charles. Just knowing about it was good enough. Besides, no one would have believed him. Ben Tyler with a purple belt!

As he walked out onto the playground at recess, he noticed everything: the hard tufts of grass under his feet, the wet smell of earthworms after last night's rain, the blue-white sky. This is a special day, Ben thought, as he drove his baseball into the center of his mitt. I'm still me, but different somehow.

166

The belt is a symbol of what you wear inside, Sifu had said, and Ben was beginning to see what he meant. Today he felt free, as if he could jump into the air and keep right on floating up and over the school. Like Sifu said, *It's okay to be Ben Tyler,* Ben Tyler who happened to hate fighting, but could do it if he had to.

Boyd leaned against his usual tree trunk almost as if he had become part of it, a fungus growing out of the bark. Ben noticed the scowl on his face and for a minute even felt sorry for him.

As Ben passed by him with Patrick and Charles, Boyd spit on the ground and moved away from the tree.

"Okay, Tyler. I've waited long enough," Boyd said coming close to Ben. "This time you won't catch me off guard."

The way he shifted from one foot to the other told Ben he wasn't as cocky as he had been before. His eyes darted nervously from side to side and never rested on Ben.

"You'd better get out of the way," Boyd said to Charles.

"I have better things to do than fight with you," Ben said. "Find someone else."

Charles and Patrick stepped out of the way as Boyd moved even closer.

"Are you sure you want to do this?" Ben asked,

remembering Mike at the restaurant. "I might beat you worse than I did before; I've learned a lot of new things since then." He hadn't really, but he could make up something if necessary.

Boyd looked at Patrick and Charles, then seemed to renew his courage. "Everyone knows I'm tougher than you, Tyler."

Ben's hand went automatically to his stomach, but to his own surprise he felt just fine. How did Boyd's stomach feel? he wondered. As sick as he looked?

Ben turned to walk away without answering. His friends followed.

"I can smear you," Boyd called after him. "Come back here and fight."

The sun came out from behind a cloud and warmed Ben's back as he and the others continued toward the baseball diamond. It's so simple, Ben thought walking on. Why can't he understand? I DON'T LIKE TO FIGHT!

Finally, Boyd screeched, "Tyler, you're asking for it!" Boyd's voice cracked as if he were about to cry.

I've got to see this, Ben thought, and he turned around in time to see Boyd drive his bare fist into the trunk of his favorite tree.

"Gees!" Charles gasped. "What'd he do that for?"

168

Ben watched in disbelief as Boyd cradled his hand against his chest and howled. Everyone on the playground turned around. Some of the kids laughed.

Ben stood for a long time silently staring at Boyd. Could that really be the same kid who had made him swallow mud? The same kid who had called him names and ruined his life for a whole year? It seemed impossible. All those stomachaches, the worrying, the plans that never worked, all because of a skinny kid who smelled like turnips.

Ben stood staring until a teacher led Boyd into the school with her arm around his shoulder. He'll probably tell the principal I did it, Ben thought, that I somehow took a tree and hit him with it.

Self Esteem